MW01716074

IN THE EYES OF A KILLER

Mamie Jean Calvert

Copyright © 2024 by

Mamie Jean Calvert

Ambra Productions LLC

All Rights Reserved. No part of this book may be reproduced or transmitted in any form or by any means, electronic or mechanical, including photocopying, recording, or by any information storage and retrieval system, without the written permission of the publisher except in the case of brief quotations, or except where permitted by law.

First edition February 2024

ISBN: 978-1-7361994-4-2

The information contained in this book is intended to be for entertainment only.

Edited by Judy Nessen

Contents

PART 1

DEDICATION

This book is dedicated to my oldest grandson, Dominick Battiato, whose extraordinary brilliance, kindness, and generosity illuminate our lives. He has a rapid response in time of need to his entire family and friends. He has an MBA degree and is certified in epidemiology and nutrition. A diehard Raiders fan, it is easy to buy him presents.

With his beautiful wife Missy and their son Kai, they reside in Southern California. The house is filled with love, along with their three Huskies that playfully break the rules.

Dominick loves his fast cars, and when the day is over you will find him in his gym working out. I thank him for all the help he has given me and for doing the amazing cover of this book.

To Rent or Buy the Movie In the Eyes of a Killer, Please Visit:

intheeyesofakiller.vhx.tv/products/in-the-eyes-of-a-killer

Chapter 1

Three men walk down a long, dark corridor. In the middle is prisoner Terrence Lee Horton, a man in his mid-forties with one striking feature: his eyes. One dark brown, the other, piercing blue—together they create a very disturbing presence. Flanking Horton are two prison guards; a priest walks behind them. They enter the execution room; a metal table sits in the center. The warden, a tall, attractive man with a stern look on his face, and the prison doctor, dressed in white, stand to the side. As the guards lead Horton to the table, he stops in front of the glass mirror and stares, clearly aware there are people in a room on the other side. Inside the room are several of the victims' family members, the press, and prison officials, waiting, watching. The witnesses grow increasingly uncomfortable. One woman, pretty, with long, dark hair, there for her sister, feels Horton's evil stare is directed right at her; she jumps. A sketch artist works on the scene on his artist's pad. Horton continues to glare into the glass, even when the warden motions for the guards to move him into position. As the doctor and guards prepare the table, the warden speaks: "Terrence Lee Horton, you have been duly convicted by the state of California for the rape and murder of Ann Miller, Carrie McCall, Joanne Wilson, Chelsea Joy, and Laura Jean. Judgment has been passed that you be executed for these crimes. Do you have any final words?"

The chilling expression on Horton's face does not change as he continues to stare through the glass. "There are more. And I'll take them to my grave."

The warden signals to the guards to put the prisoner in place. As Horton lies on the table, a guard straps his arms to the table and locks the ankle chains in place. As the final strap is secured, the doctor moves to the prisoner, swabs his heavily tattooed arm with alcohol, and inserts the canula. The warden checks his pocket watch. In the viewing room, the witnesses anxiously wait. A wall clock strikes 12. The warden confirms the time on his watch and nods. A machine purrs to life; solution runs through the clear tubes into Horton's arm. He begins to lose consciousness; however, he continues his look of controlled insanity and hatred until his breathing slows and finally stops. All that can be heard is the sound of a flatline tone on the monitor.

In the viewing room, one person quietly sobs; the others remain quiet and still. In the execution room, the doctor listens to Horton's heart with a stethoscope and nods to the warden, who motions for the guards to take the body away. One guard whispers, "I don't get this guy—someone like him donating organs?" The other guard whispers back, "The asshole probably thinks he'll live forever." The warden, overhearing this, simply says "Gentlemen." The guards react to the "scolding" and quicken their pace. On the way out, one guard closes the black viewing room curtain.

Chapter 2

In a dimly lit lecture hall filled with attentive students, horrific images of murders are projected onto a screen via PowerPoint.

"What is evil? How is it created? And why does it exist?" Professor Jack Newman, a very handsome man with striking blue eyes, controls the show with a remote as he addresses the class. "In order to understand evil, many cultures attribute it to inherent social conditions, a person's upbringing. Others blame genetics, claiming we are born with it. Most religions, however, prefer to ascribe evil to a presence, a being. You've all heard it ... 'the devil made me do it.'" The students laugh. He clicks the remote; a gory murder scene covers the screen. "Son of Sam, Charles Manson, take your pick. Right now, today, for every 100 people in America, one is a clinical psychopath."

One student, who has been listening intently, adjusts his glasses. “That’s a pretty pessimistic opinion of society, don’t you think, Professor?”

“You don’t see the world as I do, Ryan.” The class chuckles, uneasily. “Besides, it’s not opinion, it’s fact. Psychopaths in general harbor immense anger. The majority of psychopaths find pleasure enough in just fantasizing the sufferings of those who annoy them. Those are the ones who walk amongst us, unnoticed.” The class shuffles uncomfortably as faces of normal, everyday people flash on the screen. He continues: “Studies indicate that they simply do not feel nor can they understand the sufferings of others.” His watch beeps. “When we meet again, we will discuss ... the devil.”

The students collect their books and quickly file out. Jack moves to his desk. He arranges the items on his desk without looking, then opens a book. He seems to be reading in the dark as he runs his hands over the pages. He hears a click as the overhead light goes on. Reacting to the sound, not the light, he cocks his head.

“Discuss the devil? You trying to make education fun, Professor?” Gwen Ward, an attractive blonde woman in her early thirties, steps into the room.

“Well, no one fell asleep. How do you keep them awake in your psychology classes?”

“I talk about penis envy.” Jack smiles.” Come on, let’s go for a walk.”

Jack reaches beside his desk and picks up a white cane; with a click the cane flips open. Gwen moves close; Jack takes her arm. “After you, Professor. We’ll bump into less walls that way.”

Chapter 3

It's a beautiful fall day; brightly colored leaves blow in the wind. Students mill around the campus. Gwen and Jack, in the middle of their stroll, walk arm in arm, Jack carrying his white cane.

"Did our friend the good doctor call?" Gwen asks.

"He calls me every day."

Gwen pauses for a moment, thinking Jack will continue, but he doesn't. "Sam just wants us to be happy."

"We are happy."

"Okay. Happier."

Jack changes the subject. "My favorite time of the year. Seeing the leaves turn color—such beauty."

Gwen plays along. "And you see this?"

"In a way."

“I’m meeting a friend, sweetie, see you tonight?”

“I hope so.”

Gwen kisses Jack and starts to walk off. He pulls her back for one last kiss. He smiles, then lets go of her. Using his white cane, he starts walking back toward the building.

Chapter 4

Gwen and her friend Sally sit on the patio drinking coffee. Gwen chews on a candy bar. Curious, Sally asks, "How did you survive before you met Jack? Candy bars? You're lucky you're marrying a man who can cook—and lucky he's blind."

"Lucky?"

"All I know is, if I had a blind guy, I'd want to keep him that way. I'd save a fortune on cosmetics. So have you decided where the wedding's going to be?"

"Since neither of us have family in the area, Jack is thinking Vegas. He's somehow got it in his head he wants to be married by Elvis."

"An Elvis impersonator? Oh, my God, are you serious?"

"Jack is." Gwen takes a sip of coffee.

Sally is dumbfounded. "Elvis? I would scream!"

Chapter 5

A movie plays on a TV screen. A frightened woman screams as she runs through a dark cornfield, terrified, her breathing rapid, eyes darting. She turns, and she is nose-to-nose with the face of terror: a handsome blonde psychopath holding a butcher knife. The woman gasps, but she is too terrified to move. She finally turns and runs. The killer bellows with sadistic laughter. The woman races faster through the field, trying to escape. She can't. She tries to run in a different direction, but she sees the killer now right in front of her. Paralyzed with fear, she is backed into a tree. The psychopath raises his bloody implement of murder and mayhem. Terrified, frightened, the woman screams again.

Chapter 6

A large TV hangs on the wall of the den. A slasher movie is playing, with a woman being chased through a cornfield. Jack listens and laughs at the ridiculous sounds coming from the television set. Everything is neat and orderly in Jack's kitchen, where he is preparing dinner. As the movie's screaming and suspenseful music continues, he reaches into a cabinet and takes out a large pot. At the sink, he runs water, filling the pot and testing the level with his finger; he then sets it on the stove and turns on the gas. He finds the spaghetti and sauce ingredients, then goes back to listening to the TV. The slasher movie is still on; the woman screams and runs for her life, the killer right behind her. Jack laughs.

Gwen enters the dining room, carrying an armful of groceries and flowers. She smiles, seeing the perfectly set table; then she hears the filtered sounds of screaming coming from the den. Her smile fades; she heads to the kitchen and sets the groceries on the counter. She kisses Jack's cheek.

On the TV, the killer has caught up to his victim and slashes away. Gwen is disgusted. "How can you stand watching this?"

"Actually, it's radio to me, Gwen. I'm trying to prepare for my next lecture—Satan."

"Oh … kay. Well, prepare it some other time. Not before dinner." Gwen grabs the remote and turns the TV off.

Jack teases her. "You know, for a psych teacher you really need to get over your fear of maniacs with meat cleavers—they're out there."

Gwen sighs. "Yeah, well, as long as they stay 'out there'—way out there. Let's talk about something else. Anything else. Smells good." Gwen uses a spoon to stir the sauce; she lifts some up to her face for a sniff and a little taste. She returns the spoon to the counter, an inch from where she picked it up. Jack senses this and moves the spoon back to where it started. He smiles at Gwen. She realizes what she has done. "Sorry, chef."

Jack's hands search the counter, making sure everything is in its proper place. "It's the only way I can find things."

"I'll get out of your way. It's a shame, though. You know I'd love to help. I'm a real whiz in the kitchen."

Gwen heads for the door, happy to be escaping kitchen chores. The moment she is gone, Jack takes the remote, turns the TV back on, and listens to more screaming from the frightened woman.

Chapter 7

Later that evening, the remains of dinner cover the table. Candles are burnt low. Both Gwen and Jack look full and satisfied. Gwen stares at the empty dishes on the table. "I can't believe how good that was."

"Close your eyes."

"Why?"

"Just close them."

Gwen closes her eyes. After a few moments she tries to sneak a peek.

"No peeking."

Caught, Gwen closes her eyes. Jack goes to the china cupboard and opens a door, revealing a cloth-covered object. He places it in front of Gwen. "Open your eyes."

Gwen opens her eyes. Jack pulls the cloth off, revealing a near perfect clay facial sculpture of her. The detail is uncannily precise.

Gwen is speechless for a moment. “Oh, my God … it’s me. Where did you get this?”

“Actually, I made it.”

Gwen stammers. “You?! But ... how? I mean ... you can’t ...”

“I see you.” Jack touches the lines on Gwen’s forehead. “Just as I thought. I see skepticism.” Gwen forces the lines to go away. Jack grins. Still touching her forehead with one hand, he touches the forehead of the sculpture with the other, tracing it with his fingers. “See? I know your face.” Jack traces the real Gwen and the plaster Gwen simultaneously, reaching her smiling lips. “There. The same curve, with just the slightest dimple here.”

“Okay, I get ...”

Jack interrupts her. “Shhh.” He lightly closes her lips with his fingers. He traces her neck as he follows along on the plaster one. “When you get upset, this muscle tightens more than the other one. Upset ... or ... aroused." Gwen tries to speak, but again Jack shushes her and traces down to her breasts. She smiles.

Chapter 8

An Elvis ballad softly plays in the background. Jack and Gwen kiss as the light of a full moon shines through the window and envelops them in a soft glow. He moves across her semi-naked body, kissing, caressing, and exploring as only a blind man can.

"My next sculpture will be a full body … from your lips ... to your breasts ... to your stomach ... to your toes." Gwen giggles as he reaches her toes. "I knew you were the one for me the first time we did this."

Gwen chuckles. "Made love?"

"No. When we touched. The day we met."

"I remember. I dropped my books when I bumped into you. I was so embarrassed!"

"When I went to pick them up, your arm brushed against my cheek. I knew instantly we'd be sharing our lives together."

"So, you're saying ... it was love at first sight?"

"Better." Gwen smiles. Jack senses her skepticism again; he takes a scarf from the nightstand and blindfolds her. "Now tell me what you feel."

"What's this?"

"I'm going to show you how I see you."

Gwen plays along and adjusts the scarf covering her eyes. She touches Jack's face. "Okay. I feel you." She moves her hands to his chest; she puts her ear to it and listens. "I hear the sound of life." She kisses his hand. "I can taste you." Jack guides her lips to his. They kiss as he lays her down on the bed. "And what's this? I feel someone who's very happy to 'see' me."

The ballad swells.

Chapter 9

Dr. Sam Rieland sits at his desk in his office. He is quite handsome and in good shape, with light brown hair touched with grey. Gwen sits across from him, and Jack paces in front of an eye diagram.

“If I didn’t know you better, Jack, I’d think you were having second thoughts about this surgery. When I called this morning to tell you we’d found a donor, you said you had to check your calendar.”

“I’m here, aren’t I?” Jack touches Gwen. “We’re here.”

“All he talks about is how much he wants this, Sam. It’s just ... well ...”

Sam gently interrupts. “You know, sometimes getting what we want can be frightening.”

Jack stops pacing. “I’m not frightened.” He pauses. “Okay, tell me about the donor.”

"You can relax. He was about your age, with 20/20 vision. And healthy."

"Apparently not so healthy—he's dead, isn't he?"

"The eyes are healthy. That's all we're concerned about." Sam looks at his desk calendar. "We can schedule the surgery for tomorrow."

"Oh ... that soon?"

"Jack, we've talked about this. When eyes become available, we've got to move quickly."

"It's just hard to imagine this is going to work."

"This will work, Jack. I wouldn't recommend it otherwise. After six years of testing, we're convinced we can move on to the next level."

"Yeah, but those tests were done on rats. And what about all the research finding cellular memory in heart and other organ donor recipients?"

"Cellular memory?" Gwen is curious.

"It's not what it sounds like. You're not picking up the memories of the donor—it means that the cell is remembering functioning in the body. That's all."

"I've read stuff, Sam, there's other theories ..."

"All bogus. You want facts? Donor recipients tend to live long, rich lives without setbacks. This is a real chance for you, Jack"

Jack turns away as Gwen and Sam exchange frustrated looks.

"I just don't know ..."

"Jack, this isn't something new. We've talked about this for months. You even knew I was inviting the press here today. They're outside, waiting to meet you, waiting for the big announcement."

Jack remains silent, his back to them. Gwen moves to him and touches his face, speaking softly. "Sweetheart, isn't this what you always hoped for? With this you have a chance to finally have your sight again."

Jack feels queasy. "I need to get some air." He leaves the office.

"He'll be okay … it's just pre-op jitters. Everyone gets them. Right?"

"Gwen, it could be another six months or a year, or longer, before we get another match. I thought we were all in agreement. If the opportunity came up, we would move on it. Well, it's here."

Gwen moves to the window, concern on her face. "How do we know the diabetes won't cause a problem with the new eyes?"

"His diabetes has been under control for years. The damage was done before he'd been diagnosed properly."

Gwen looks out the window. "Oh, my God!" She rushes out of the office.

Chapter 10

Jack tries to cross the road in an attempt to escape a group of reporters with video cameras who have pursued him to the edge of the street.

A reporter yells out, "Hey, take it easy, buddy, we just want to ask you a couple of questions."

"I've got nothing to say!"

Gwen hurries from the medical building and pushes her way through the reporters. "Jack, it's okay, I'm coming to get you."

As she steps off the curb, a reporter distracts her. "Hey, are you his wife? Is he the guy who's going to have the transplant? We just need a sound bite for the news."

"Leave him alone! He's not ready!" Suddenly there's the sound of screeching brakes. Gwen spins to see a 2007 blue Chrysler stop just short of her. The newsmen do nothing to help, but they roll their cameras.

The driver yells, “What are you, blind?!”

Gwen, flustered, makes her way to the other side of the road with Jack. “Are you okay, Jack?”

“I’m fine. What were you trying to do?”

Both are relieved to be alive and together. Jack looks back toward the group of reporters. “Let’s go home.”

Chapter 11

Jack expertly chops vegetables for dinner, his back to Gwen, who gently moves the sculpture he made of her to the counter and sits down. She studies the detail. “I feel like I’m looking in a mirror—this is really amazing, Jack.” She turns to him. “Imagine what you’ll be able to do once you can see.”

Jack is silent. Gwen goes to him and looks closely at his face. He continues chopping vegetables. Chop chop chop. Gwen waits; Jack senses that she is there. “You know, I do okay. As a matter of fact, I think I’m happier now than when I could see. I don’t take anything for granted anymore. I must be crazy to even be considering doing this.”

Gwen gently strokes his hair. “You’ll be okay.”

Jack is agitated by now. “I can get to work on the bus. I can support myself. I can cook. I can clean. I shouldn’t have to prove that to you.”

"Jack, you don't ..."

"Just in this room alone—I can find things faster than anyone with eyes." He grabs his white cane and starts pointing with it. "There's the stove. The medium button is here." He punches the medium button with his cane, on and off. "The sink is here. Hot. Cold. The toaster is here." He swings the cane around and hits the sculpture; it falls to the floor and shatters. He is silent, then drops to his knees and frantically tries to pick up the pieces.

"Jack, it's okay."

Jack cuts himself on one of the broken pieces. Gwen grabs a wet cloth, cleans his cut hand and tries to soothe him. "Honey, it's okay. You can make another one."

"No. No, I can't. I can't protect you." He tries to reach for more pieces, but she pulls his hand back.

"What! It's not me, Jack."

"Today this could have been you, because of me. You look out for me, Gwen. I need ... I need to look out for you."

The broken pieces of sculpture lay scattered on the floor. A drop of blood lands on an eye socket.

Chapter 12

Dr. Sam Rieland and an assistant, along with an operating room staff, will conduct the eye transplant surgery on Jack as a camera crew documents the procedure. Sam seems to relish the attention.

As the procedure unfolds:

- Jack is prepped for surgery.
- A doctor sets up a camera and monitor.
- In the waiting room, Gwen watches the clock and paces.
- A set of clamps keep Jack's eyes wide open.
- Sam removes Jack's original eyes.

The assistant, Doctor Tris, brings in a solution-filled jar with a pair of eyes inside. Sam whispers to him: "They're two different colors."

"I know. I checked, they're from the same donor."

"Are we going to have a legal problem with this, Doctor?"

"His form stated eye color didn't matter."

Sam proceeds with the surgery; when it's over, he looks down at Jack, who is out. "At least he'll see."

All of the doctors leave the room. Jack is soundly sleeping.

Chapter 13

Jack lies in bed. His head and eyes are bandaged. Sam moves to Jack's bedside and touches him gently on the shoulder. "Jack, you awake?"

Jack is drowsy. "Yeah."

"How do you feel?"

"Head ... hurts."

"I'd be concerned if it didn't."

"So … how'd it go?"

"I think it went very well." He pauses for a second. "I need to tell you something, Jack. We never talked about the color of the eyes."

"It didn't matter. I had Gwen note that on the form."

"We know that, that's why we proceeded with the surgery. But … you have a very special pair of eyes. It's almost like you have two sets, actually."

"You put four eyes in me?"

"We're going to get enough attention as it is. But they are unique. You've got a blue one and a brown one."

"Well ... that'll be interesting when I get my driver's license."

"At least you'll have a driver's license." Sam pats Jack's leg. "Time to meet the press." Sam moves to the door. Before opening it, he turns back to Jack. "Don't mention the headache. We're not getting paid to sell aspirin." He opens the door. "All right, gentlemen, come in and meet the future."

A camera crew and reporters enter the room. After a few questions, Jack seems to become overwhelmed. Sam notices Gwen at the doorway and decides to end the interview. "Okay, everybody, there will be plenty of time to meet our famous patient later. Let's give him some breathing room."

As the press exits, Gwen enters the room and sits next to Jack as he falls asleep.

Chapter 14

A few days later, Sam cuts the bandages off of Jack's head. Jack keeps his eyes closed for a few moments before slowly opening them. He sees a blur of colors and shapes. He makes an effort to force open his eyes, then he instantly closes them again, covering them with his hands. A beautiful nurse wearing a blue uniform hands Sam a bottle of solution. He opens one of Jack's eyes and applies the solution. "All right, Jack, let's try again. Slowly this time."

Jack tries again, blinking. He sees shapes and forms of people. "My God, it worked. I can see." He takes in the sights of the room. Gwen, a bit apprehensive, inches closer. "I see you, Gwen. I can really see you." She rushes to him and kisses him; he touches her face. "I memorized your face, but you're more beautiful than I even imagined." He pauses. "What about me? How do I look?"

Gwen covers the brown eye with her hand. "Like Brad Pitt." She then covers the blue eye. "Like George Clooney." She smiles, looking at the whole Jack. "I think I could get used to this. But now you need to get some rest."

Sam, impressed with himself, looks back at the camera crew and smiles.

Chapter 15

A killer stalks a woman through a fog covered field. The frightened woman glances over her shoulder, then runs. The killer chases, his heavy breathing being the dominant sound. He reaches out, grabs her, spins her around. It's Gwen! She struggles, then falls. The killer's hands go around her neck. Her legs flail about. Then darkness.

Chapter 16

Jack, sitting by the pool in the backyard, watches the sunset. He wears special sunglasses that wrap around his eyes. “Come on. You’re going to miss it!”

Gwen comes out of the house, carrying two glasses and a bottle of champagne. She looks to the sky. “It is beautiful, isn’t it.”

“I had forgotten just how beautiful.”

Gwen pops the cork. “I know you don’t usually drink, but this is worth celebrating.” She pours the champagne and hands a glass to Jack.

“I don’t think I’ll ever get tired of watching the sunset again.”

“To sunsets.” They toast.

Jack takes off his sunglasses, revealing those eyes. He stares intensely toward the sun for the first time. He actually appears somewhat demented. As he stares, he takes a gulp of champagne, nearly emptying the glass.

"Hey, take it easy, cowboy. It's only been a couple days. Sam said to keep the glasses on."

"Oh ... yeah." Jack slips the sunglasses back on, then finishes his champagne with one more gulp. He sets the empty glass down. Gwen looks at it, incredulously. "I don't want to wait—let's get married now. Let's just do it."

Gwen hesitates. "Of course I want to … but you know, I've got to make arrangements."

"You've got vacation time due. Besides, it'll be good for your psych classes to learn how to deal with separation anxiety." Gwen meets his look, and his smile. She nods.

Chapter 17

In the university lecture hall, Gwen finishes her lecture to the class. "Incidents of high stress will drive some to extreme behavior. No example reflects this better than that of a psychopath, who will lose control of all rational thinking and therefore all control under extreme duress." She looks at the clock; it's the top of the hour. "Read chapter 14 on Sigmund Freud, and be prepared for a quiz." The students groan.

Jack, wearing his sunglasses, enters and waits by the door as the class leaves. He pats a student on the back; "Take Davis down."

Gwen finally notices him. "This is a nice surprise."

Jack walks into the classroom as the students continue to file out. "I thought we could talk."

"Yeah? About what."

"I thought we could talk about marriage."

Gwen smiles. “How about talking about our honeymoon.”

“All right. So what’d ya got?”

Gwen pulls out two brochures from a stack on her desk, one for Tahiti and one for the Caribbean. “Depends on how far away you want to go. I was thinking ...”

Jack notices the corner of a brochure buried in the pile. His eyes move to the brochure and he pulls it out—the Lighthouse Resort. “What’s this?”

Gwen takes it and looks at it. “I’m not sure how this even got in here.” She turns it over. “Oh, that’s right. I wrote the name of a restaurant on it—the one the travel agent told us to try if we go to Hawaii.”

Gwen starts to toss the brochure away, but Jack stops her. “I like this. It looks good.”

Gwen looks at the brochure. “The Lighthouse Resort? It’s in the Delta region, not far from here.”

“See if we can get a reservation.”

“Really? We always talked about a tropical paradise.”

Jack gives her a strange smile. “As long as we’re together.”

She looks at the brochure again, a quizzical expression on her face.

Chapter 18

Jack wears a dark suit and Gwen wears a short white wedding dress and long veil. They have a small wedding under a big oak tree. They are married by an Elvis impersonator, dressed in all white with a long red scarf hanging around his neck.

A small group of friends attends; they make an arch for Jack and Gwen to run under. The Elvis impersonator plays the guitar in the background, singing, "I left my heart and heading to the Delta, heading for the Delta shores." Louis picks up Gwen and carries her off to their honeymoon.

Chapter 19

Jack and Gwen stand by the railing of the upper deck of a ferry, looking toward the Lighthouse Resort. He wears his sunglasses.

"There it is, Jack."

"Pretty as a picture. And the best thing is, we'll practically have the island to ourselves."

"I suppose that's the advantage to taking a honeymoon off season."

Jack turns to survey the near empty deck of the ferry. The only people on board are the crew and a half dozen other passengers. Leaning against the railing next to Gwen is a young man with long dark hair, probably in his 20s. "Not many people on board today. Are you staying at the resort?"

"No, I work there. This is how it is this time of year. During the summer this boat makes three trips a day—filled to capacity. Come the end of the year, she only makes one trip a day. I'm Bobby, by the way. I'm a waiter at the resort restaurant."

"Nice to meet you, Bobby. I'm sure we'll see you there." Gwen turns to Jack, a smile on her face. "That means we're going to have a lot of alone time. I'm excited."

Jack speaks quietly to her. "I had a feeling he wasn't a guest."

"Why?"

"Notice the boots. Work boots—and he's alone."

"Aren't you the observant one."

"My new hobby. People watching." He motions with his head. "Tell me what you see."

Gwen looks at the passengers. "A middle-aged woman with red hair reading a book."

Jack corrects her. "A woman who lives on the island, works at the resort. She makes this trip often, so often she's bored with it. That's why she's reading—and she's interested in dark things, the macabre. Notice the book: *Murder, Mayhem and Serial Killers*. Not your normal 'chick lit' fare." He motions to a couple standing by the railing on the other side of the deck. “Now, there’s a happy couple.” He’s a bit of a nerd who holds, and is very protective of, a metal detector. She’s a bit of a nag, as she berates him about bringing his stupid toy. “Well ... maybe not so happy. Let’s try not to sit near them at dinner.”

The ferry whistle sounds.

Chapter 20

Jack, Gwen, and others disembark from the ferry. The book lady also leaves, but she walks past everyone on her way to the resort.

Waiting to greet the group of tourists and vacationers is Clarence Butcher, a very tall, good looking Black man, who is a tour guide and resort rep. With him, off to the side, is middle-aged resort boat wrangler known simply as Witt, bald and always riding around in his yellow golf cart. Also standing there is Sheriff Whitman, slim and stern looking; he clearly has an agenda as he closely watches anyone new to the island.

Clarence stops the guests on the dock. “Welcome to the Delta’s finest and most secluded couple’s destination: The Lighthouse Resort.”

Jack lowers his sunglasses. His eyes search the area. It all looks familiar to him.

Clarence continues. “We have created an environment free from distractions, where the focus can be on each other ... the outside world can fade into the horizon. You might as well turn those cell phones off, they don’t work here.”

Jack’s gaze moves to a pay phone booth at the end of the dock. Gwen notices he is distracted and quietly asks, “What’s the matter?”

“Nothing. Just a feeling ... that I’ve been here ...”

Their attention again turns to Clarence. “Follow me, folks, and I’ll show y’all to your bungalows.” He indicates a couple points of interest as he leads the group away. As Jack and Gwen pass the sheriff, he looks at Jack with suspicion. Jack sees this and puts his sunglasses back on, concealing his eyes.

The metal detector man, anxious to get away from his wife, pushes past Jack and goes up to Clarence. “I’m Ned Bigler. I’m here with my wife. I heard there might be some buried treasure here.”

Clarence smiles. “Well now, there is some folklore ’bout all that but nothing’s been found, which is why I still work for a living.”

The small crowd laughs. Bigler holds up his metal detector. “I’m hoping to find some”

“Good luck to you, sir.”

Bigler’s wife, Mamie, is very annoyed. “Where can you get a drink around here?”

Clarence chuckles. “You folks follow me and I’ll show you.”

The crowd follows Clarence and divert to their respective lodgings.

Jack and Gwen arrive at their vacation bungalow and survey the surroundings. Gwen is impressed. “I have to admit, maybe the Delta was a good idea!”

Jack is less impressed. “No TV.”

Gwen sees a record player and a small stack of record albums. She turns on the record player and moves over to Jack, dancing around playfully. They share a long kiss.

Chapter 21

The Lighthouse Resort restaurant's patio looks out onto the docks, where illuminated houseboats float by in the marina. Gwen and Jack sit at a patio table. He drinks whiskey on the rocks; she sips wine. Jack toasts Gwen: "To a new life—where everything will be different."

Gwen takes a sip. Concerned, she watches Jack down his drink. "I'm surprised to see you drinking—especially whiskey. Do you think that's such a good idea?"

"You worry too much. I never noticed that about you before. You need to let your hair down." Jack signals for another drink to the waiter, the young man they saw on the ferry.

Gwen smiles, feeling comforted by this old habit. She puts her hand on Jack's. "I love you."

The waiter comes over to the table. "Here's your drink, sir." Jack looks up; the waiter, seeing his eyes, reacts nervously, then catches himself. “Your food should be ready. I’ll ... go check on it.”

Gwen again says ‘I love you’ to Jack. She follows his unflinching gaze as he stares at a beautiful, large chested woman having dinner with her boyfriend at a nearby table. A disturbing vision enters his head: Like a scene out of *Psycho*, a man’s hand yanks open a shower curtain, revealing a lovely, naked woman standing under the spray. The tile on the wall behind her has distinctive decals. The hands grab her and push her against the wall. One hand holds a knife to her throat. The other hand runs its fingers through her wet, soapy hair. “Beautiful hair—the first thing I noticed when I saw you.” The hand yanks her hair. She screams as he cuts, the knife separating her beautiful hair from her skull. Her arms flail, hitting the man.

The waiter leans in with Jack’s plate of food. Jack slaps it away, reacting to the vision he’s just had. The crash of the plate jars him back to reality.

Every eye in the place is on him now. In an attempt to reorient himself, he looks around the room. He sees Bigler and his wife Mamie, staring. At the bar is Congressman Edward Donalds, a very handsome man, and his trophy wife, Kari, both staring. At another table is Sheriff Whitman; Gretchen, the book lady from the ferry, is serving him a drink from behind the bar. Both stare. The waiter quickly drops to his knees to clean up the mess.

“Jack, are you okay?”

“I just need a drink …”

Chapter 22

Jack has his arm around Gwen as they walk on the dock outside the restaurant. He's drunkenly singing a drinking song, "Show Me the Way to Go Home."

Gwen tries to have a good time, despite what happened. "I do hope you remember this is our honeymoon, Mr. Jack … Daniels."

"Of course I do. Why do you think I was celebrating?" Gwen is silent; Jack is oblivious to her mood. "I have big plans for us, honey. I ordered champagne. It should be waiting for us when we get back to our bungalow."

In the bungalow, Gwen sits on the bed, wearing a beautiful negligee, drinking champagne. Annoyed, she looks toward the bathroom.

Jack's head is in the toilet; he is retching and throwing up. Finished, he washes his face with cold water and looks in the mirror. He quietly talks to his reflection: “What’s your problem, Jack? You didn’t used to be such a jerk.” When he drops his head down to rinse his face again, he looks over to the shower. Shocked, he realizes the tile has the same distinct pattern as the tile in his vision at the restaurant. He lifts his head, stares at the shower, then throws up again. He has another vision: blood washing down the shower drain.

Chapter 23

The next morning, Gwen is at the dining room table, having a cup of coffee. Jack, wearing sunglasses, comes in. “Good morning, sunshine. Feeling better today?”

Jack pours himself a cup of coffee, his hands shaky. Gwen notices, but says nothing. “Yeah, I guess so. What exactly happened to me last night?”

“You mean, when Jekyll became Hyde?”

“Was I that bad?”

Gwen gently pats his hand, trying to calm the trembling. “You were celebrating.”

“Remind me not to celebrate anymore.”

“You’ll be okay. Let’s just forget about last night, and have a fun day exploring the island.”

“I’d rather explore you!” With a devilish smile, Jack pulls Gwen close, exploring her body. The passion quickly ignites. He carries her to the table.

They push the flower centerpiece off. He runs his fingers through her hair. "Beautiful hair." He sucks on her ear, then her neck, and works his way down her body. This is very different from the way they've made love before. This time, he is driving the exchange with primal lust and even a hint of angry, reckless passion. Clothes do not get removed; they get torn from the body. Lips and flesh do not get kissed; they get sucked and bitten. Gwen is surprised and even intrigued; she does not resist this hedonistic exchange.

Jack falls back onto a chair, exhausted, satisfied. Gwen, too, is satisfied—and confused.

Chapter 24

Jack, wearing sunglasses, chases Gwen through the trees on a shoreline trail. She laughs as he pretends to catch her, then lets her get away. He falls off as she continues to run. She pauses and returns to see him standing by a distinctive tree, staring at the ground in a peculiar way. He squats down and traces his finger in the dirt.

"Lose something?"

"No ... I think I found something."

"What?"

"I don't know." Jack continues to touch the ground, almost caressing the soil. Gwen is puzzled as she watches his odd conduct. He stands up, taking one last look at the spot on the ground. "Let's go." He walks off toward the beach. She looks back at the spot of ground and then follows him.

They find a nice spot to have a picnic. Gwen relaxes on a blanket, soaking up the warm weather.

Jack removes his sunglasses and sits next to her, looking somber. He stares blankly at the water. “I’ve been having bad dreams—ever since the operation.” Gwen sits up, paying attention to what Jack is saying. “There’s this guy. He’s always with a woman. It gets kind of rough—maybe she likes it, I’m not sure, but he’s definitely in charge.”

“Who is he?”

“I don’t know. I can only see his hands ... and the things he does ... the terrible things he does.” Jack stares out at the water, his mind somewhere else. Gwen watches him, concerned.

Chapter 25

Their day at the beach over, they go to the Lighthouse Resort restaurant. Gwen spots a table and moves toward it, but Jack heads straight to the bar. Gwen almost calls to him, then relents and follows.

At the bar, Sheriff Whitman is drinking and laughing with Ed Donalds and Kari. When Jack arrives at the bar and sees the sheriff, he immediately puts on his sunglasses, just as Gwen catches up. “Are we incognito?” she teases.

“A little too much sun today, I guess. Feels better this way.” Gretchen approaches from the business side of the bar to take their order. “Whiskey on the rocks. White wine for the lady.”

“Hello there! Welcome to the party! I’m Ed Donalds. This is my wife, Kari.”

Jack nods, watching them without speaking, looking more at Kari's breasts than hearing what Donalds is saying.

"Congressman Donalds, isn't it?" Gwen asks.

"Not tonight, not here. It's just Ed. One of the people."

Kari, teasingly, sets him straight. "One of the drunk people."

"Well, Ed, I'm Gwen, and this is my husband, Jack. Nice to meet you. Are you on your honeymoon as well?"

"That's right. Married two days ago. And they said it wouldn't last!" Ed and Kari laugh. Jack continues to leer at Kari. Gretchen serves Jack and Gwen their drinks.

The sheriff holds up his drink. "You got yourself a keeper this time, Ed. Here's to a happy union." They all toast.

Gwen turns to Ed. "I'm surprised we got the Grand Bungalow with you being newlyweds, too."

"I brought my own bungalow—a yacht. I never leave home without it."

"First time here, Ed?"

"No. I've been coming here for ... how long now, Gretchen. Ten years?"

"Yep. Ever since the Horton murders."

Gwen stammers. "I'm … I'm sorry, someone was murdered here?"

The sheriff tries to correct Gretchen: "No one's ever died on this island."

Gretchen won't let it go. "That's right, they just go missing. It was three in one weekend, as I recall."

The sheriff grumbles. "Ancient history."

"Oh ... maybe you're right. That was ten years ago." Her sarcasm is obvious. But the sheriff relaxes, satisfied he's soothed the beast. Then Gretchen gets in a final dig: "And they're STILL missing."

The sheriff shoots Gretchen a look that she brushes off. Ed tries to play peacemaker. "Gretchen, be a doll and bring a round for everyone, on me, the sheriff included. This is a night for celebration." Gretchen walks away. Ed looks at Jack and Gwen. "Nice girl, but reads too many mysteries."

Gwen politely smiles. Jack notices a necklace nestled between Kari's ample breasts. "Nice necklace you got there, Kari."

Gwen sees Jack's focus and tries to prevent an embarrassing scene. "Yes, it is beautiful."

"Oh, thank you. Ed gave it to me." Kari shows off her necklace and her impressive cleavage.

"Nice," Jack mutters, staring at her breasts. Gwen casts a sideways glance at him.

As the drinks arrive, Ed brags some more. "I knew this was the girl for me the moment I saw her."

Jack, still staring: "I can see why." He drains his drink. Gwen watches, disapprovingly. Ed and Kari carry on, playfully kissing each other.

Gwen turns away, speaking quietly to Jack. "Will you behave yourself and slow down on the drinking? We don't want a repeat of last night."

"It's a celebration, right?"

"I thought we weren't going to celebrate anymore."

"There's plenty of time to not celebrate when we get home. Loosen up, will you?" Jack slaps the bar and takes off his sunglasses, revealing those eyes. “Two more, straight up this time.”

Suddenly Jack starts tidying up anything he can find on the bar, almost manically. Gwen notices this, then sees the sheriff has noticed, too. She whispers, “Jack, just let it go.” He ignores her. The sheriff stares more and more at Jack.

Chapter 26

Gwen sits beside the bungalow pool and reads the newspaper as she sips coffee. The patio door opens and an aloof Jack, in his robe and wearing his sunglasses, walks over to a table. He picks up a section of the newspaper and sits next to Gwen.

"How did you sleep last night?" Gwen is silent. "What's wrong?"

Gwen looks at him for a moment and chooses her words carefully. "It's our honeymoon. You get drunk every night, make an ass out of yourself, then come back here and pass out. What's wrong with me? What's wrong with you?" Jack nervously starts to straighten items on the table, like he did at the restaurant. He shuffles through the newspaper, which frustrates Gwen. "Will you stop that and listen to me?!" Jack stops and looks at her. She is trying to calm down, but she is not succeeding.

"We are on our honeymoon and I want us to have some fun together!"

"If you want to have fun, why don't we go out on a boat."

Gwen pauses for a moment. "Well, all right. But I'm not ready yet."

"Then I'll go check it out." Jack tosses the paper. He stares at Gwen for a moment before walking off, leaving her speechless.

Chapter 27

At the dock, Kari Donalds, in a revealing bikini, sunbathes on the upper deck of her yacht. Jack slows to take in the scenery. She notices Jack and lowers her sunglasses to check him out. She smiles slyly and waves her fingers in a seductive hello. Ed walks onto the deck and stares at Jack. Jack's expression hardens at the interruption, then he continues walking.

His walk eventually leads him to an old dock, an area used by the locals, not tourists. Further down the dock, Grady, a man in his sixties, watches Jack like a hawk from inside his shop. Jack walks into the shop and takes off his sunglasses. "Hey, Pops, I understand you got boats for rent."

Grady obviously doesn't appreciate being called 'Pops.' "Sure, they're for rent. Need them to come back, though. We share this here waterway with that fancy resort, and one of their guests drowning in my boat is trouble I don't need."

"How much for this one?" Jack points to a fancy speedboat.

"Seventy-five dollars a day."

Jack tosses several bills onto the counter. Grady stares at him for a moment, then grabs a key from the cabinet behind the counter. "Just try not to drown out there, I don't need no sheriff grillin' my ass." Jack heads to the boat. Grady watches as Jack gets in and shoots him a smug look. "Smart ass."

Jack revs the engine, building up speed as he races through the marina. He rounds a bend and passes the bungalow. Gwen, still by the pool, sees him. As he passes, he gives her a quick wave. She throws down her sunglasses and storms back into the house.

Jack speeds through the Delta. After a few moments he notices a place to dock on shore and pilots the boat in that direction. He ties off the boat and stands on the North Shore trail, looking at the same spot of loose dirt under the distinctive tree he and Gwen were at earlier. At the foot of the tree, he surveys the area. He squats down and touches the dirt. Then he stands up, eyes still on the ground, obsessed with the grave-like dirt. He removes his sunglasses and stares with those intense eyes.

As Jack begins to leave, he comes face to face with Ned Bigler, the metal detector guy. Jack lets out a gasp, scaring Bigler. “Holy shit, you scared me half to death!”

“What are you doing?”

Bigler looks around, baffled. “What?”

“What are you doing here right now?” Jack glares at Bigler. Those eyes are back, brighter than usual—penetrating, threatening.

Bigler swallows hard. “I was just checking along the trail for metal. You know, rings, watches, coins, the sort of things people lose. You’d be surprised ...” Bigler activates the metal detector and immediately gets a signal. He looks toward the ground in front of the old tree. “There might be something over there ...” Bigler sees the look on Jack’s face and decides to back off.

“I think you’d be better sticking closer to the resort.” Jack’s eyes burn a hole through Bigler, who nervously moves on. Jack waits until he is alone, then looks back to where the grave was. The dirt remains undisturbed.

Chapter 28

While Jack is out on the speedboat, Gwen walks to the marina and the island's only phone booth. She inserts a few coins, then dials and waits for the call to connect. "Dr. Sam Rieland, please. Tell him it's Gwen Newman—it's important." She gazes around while waiting and sees a local man gutting a large fish. Squeamish, she turns away just as Sam comes on the line.

"Gwen, how's my star patient doing?"

"Well, that's just it ..."

While Sam talks on the phone from his office, he's holding a magazine with a picture of himself on the cover and a headline "New Visionary Brings Gift of Sight." He smiles to himself, then interrupts Gwen. "You'd better tell Jack to enjoy his privacy while he still has it—he's been making quite a stir with the press."

“Sam, there may be a problem. Jack’s been having ... complications.”

Sam puts down the magazine. “What type of complications?”

“Mood shifts, nightmares ... he’s just not acting like himself ...”

“His vision. Is he seeing all right?”

“Yes ... I don’t know ... he hasn’t said anything about that. It’s his behavior. It’s not Jack—not the Jack I know.”

Sam considers Gwen’s words, as well as his response to them. “You know, Gwen ... it’s not uncommon for an organ transplant recipient to act out of the ordinary for a time after an operation. And this represents a big change for Jack. He’s trying to adjust to seeing for the first time in years.”

“You’re not talking to a layman, Sam. I understand psychology. You know that.”

“I also know that Jack isn’t the only one who’s been under a lot of pressure lately, with this operation and all the changes. Gwen, just give him a little time to get reacquainted with everything.

He's probably putting a lot of pressure on himself to return to how he was years ago, but that's not something he'll be able to do overnight."

Gwen listens patiently. "Is there anything you can tell me about the donor? Did he drink?"

"Drink? How would I know a thing like that?"

"Jack's been drinking—a lot."

"I've never known Jack to drink much. Nothing beyond an occasional glass of wine."

"That's the thing—it isn't making any sense to me, either. Can you find something, anything, about the donor?"

"Gwen, we don't have access to personal information about the donor. Even if I could, it would be unethical for …"

"Please, just see what you can find out. I'll call you tomorrow."

"Gwen ..."

"Do it for Jack. Do it for me. I'm desperate, Sam." Gwen hangs up.

“Gwen ...” Sam hangs up the phone. Troubled over this development, he flips the magazine closed with a degree of temperament.

Gwen walks away from the phone booth. The fisherman holds up a large fish. “Fresh fish here.” Gwen reacts with disgust. He puts the fish on his makeshift counter and picks up a cleaver. Chop—the fish head falls off. Appalled, Gwen leaves.

Chapter 29

It's dark. On the dock, Jack, still wearing his sunglasses, stares at the Donalds' yacht. He climbs onboard and peers through a window into the cabin. Ed is lying on the bed; Kari stands in front of him, dancing seductively. Looking past her husband and seeing Jack out the window, she becomes more sexual in her dancing. Ed, oblivious to Jack, encourages his wife's actions.

Jack gets off the yacht and returns to the bungalow. He tosses his sunglasses down, ignoring Gwen. He takes a bottle of booze out of a cabinet and pours himself a drink.

Gwen notices his strange behavior. "What are you doing?" Jack is silent. "Are you not speaking to me now?" Jack continues to ignore her, enjoying his drink. "I think we need to have a talk." Gwen moves to the kitchen where Jack is standing. "What's going on with you, Jack?"

"I don't know what you mean." He pours himself another drink.

"And this drinking, Jack." Furious, Gwen grabs the bottle and tosses it in the sink. Jack walks away as Gwen follows him through the house. "I thought we could talk about today."

"And what about today do you want to talk about?"

"You've been acting ... very strange, Jack. Different."

"So you keep saying. Tell me, doctor, if I'm not acting like myself, then who am I acting like?"

"Like someone I've never met. Like someone I wouldn't want to meet."

Jack smiles, but Gwen's silent stare turns the condescending grin into open hostility. "A guy tries to have a little fun on his honeymoon and he turns into Mr. Fucking Hyde. Is that it? IS THAT WHAT YOU'RE TRYING TO SAY, GWEN?"

Startled at this outburst, Gwen's eyes fill with tears as she searches for a response. "It's just ... ever since you got your eyes ... it's like ... do I disappoint you that much, Jack? Do you not like what you see?"

Jack walks to the bar, gets a bottle, and pours himself another drink. "It's all about you, isn't it. I guess I should expect that from a psych teacher. Maybe I want to have a little bit of freedom—some long overdue fun."

Gwen takes the bottle away from him and tosses it in the trash. "Then why don't you go have your fun somewhere else!"

Jack grabs her and pushes her back against the wall. He holds her there, his face a mere inch from hers. His breathing is harsh. She doesn't dare breathe at all. He blinks, rubs his forehead, then eases up a bit, a subtle change. "That sounds like a good idea." He releases her; his look softens. "Stay away from me, Gwen. For your own good." He walks out of the room. She sinks to her knees and sobs.

Chapter 30

Jack, visibly agitated, enters the Lighthouse Resort restaurant. Kari and Ed, who obviously has had too much to drink, are at the end of the bar. Gretchen is behind the bar, arranging glasses.

"I have the most beautiful wife, don't I, Gretchen."

Gretchen rolls her eyes. "Yeah. Beautiful."

"I want to dance with my beautiful wife." He tries to stand, but stumbles. Kari catches him.

"Come on, baby, let's get you back to the boat. We'll do our dancing there."

Jack sits at the bar as Kari helps her husband to the door. She casts Jack a glance of recognition, which he returns.

Gretchen approaches Jack. "He was better off with the last wife. Plain as a post, but at least she didn't hiss when she smiled. What'll it be?" She hisses.

"Just give me a drink—whiskey."

Gretchen goes for the drink. Jack stares after Kari and Ed.

Outside on the dock, a sobbing Gwen is on the phone. "I don't know what's happening, Sam—the look in his eyes—for a moment, it felt like he wanted to kill me."

Sam, in his office, has a file laid out on his desk; the file includes a picture of Terrence Lee Horton. "Just calm down, Gwen. I understand how upset you are. When you come back I'll talk to Jack. I'll prescribe something to help with the mood shifts."

"I don't think he's going to come back—at least not with me. I mean ... he's not the same. I'm afraid he's going to hurt someone." She pauses for a second between sobs. "Did you find out anything about the donor?"

Sam closes Horton's file. "No. We don't need to do a witch hunt here. Maybe you can do something to help, Gwen. You have a degree in psychology, start talking to him like a psychologist—take control."

"I'll try, but he doesn't listen now."

"Maybe I should come out, we can work together. If I left now I could be there in the morning."

"Sam, really—you'd do that?"

"Try to stay calm. We'll find a way to make this right."

"Thank you, Sam."

"I'll see you in the morning." Sam hangs up. The look on his face is not the look of a friend.

Chapter 31

Elsewhere on the dock, Jack stands outside the Donalds' yacht—waiting. On the top deck Kari is drinking wine, enjoying the night sky. She notices Jack. "Ahoy there. What are you doing out this late? That wife of yours must be pretty careless."

"She's not the late-night party type. Looks like your husband isn't, either."

"Fast asleep down below, dead to the world. I've warned him about vodka. Makes him comatose."

"Damn shame. Looks like you and I have the same problem."

Kari smiles. "Well, you know what they say about mutual problems—misery loves company. Care to join me for a nightcap before I go below?"

"Sure. One last drink won't hurt anybody. Right?"

Jack climbs aboard. Kari hands him a glass of wine. "So ... did you know your wife was a stick in the mud before you married her?"

"Actually, I was blind to it. But the way I see it, now, is we only have one life ... and we should really experience everything. You agree?"

Kari notices his naughty look. This is fun for her, but only to a point. "I'd have to say that marriage has allowed me to experience more. Ed's been very good to me. Very generous."

"Sounds like an ideal arrangement—especially when he sleeps."

Kari smiles and casts Jack a sly look. She stands to refill her glass; Jack moves behind her. His breath increases as he places his hands on her hips. She smiles, but protests. "There's a time and a place for everything."

"Daddy Congressman's not going to wake up—not unless you start screaming."

"I'm not the screaming type."

"All the better."

Jack pulls Kari to him and kisses her. She pulls away. "This is really not a good idea." As she tries to move past Jack, he presses against her, kissing harder. She permits it for a moment, then pulls back. "Listen, lover boy ..." Jack kisses her again, moving his hands up the front of her blouse. She resists. "You're going to make trouble for me."

"Something tells me you're the kind of girl who likes a little trouble."

"Not when it threatens my livelihood!" She peels Jack's hands off her breasts. "Those cost me a lot of money—and you don't look like the type who can afford them."

Unfazed, Jack presses forward. Kari backs away, toward the stern of the yacht. She hits the rail and teeters, a mixture of intoxication and fear. Jack grabs for her, but instead he gets her necklace. Kari loses her balance; she screams as she falls into the water. The necklace still in his hand, Jack looks over the railing. Kari flails; the cold water takes her breath away, stifling her screams. "Help me!"

"I thought you said you weren't the screaming type."

"I can't swim!"

"With those breasts, you ought to float." Kari sinks out of sight. "Or maybe not. I'd like to have something to remember you by." He looks at the necklace in his hand. "Guess this will have to do."

Chapter 32

Back in the bungalow, Gwen sits in the shadows in the living room, waiting. She is calmer, determined, ready. Jack comes in and almost walks by before he notices her presence. "Well, well. Miss me?"

"It's three a.m., Jack."

"Now you're keeping track of my hours? How charming."

"I've been keeping track of more than that. You've become a bit of a paradox."

"Uh oh, sounds like it's shrink time."

Gwen disregards his sarcasm. "You're losing control, Jack."

"I have control." He steps up to the bar and pours a drink.

"The increased drinking. You're just trying to control … like you're losing it somehow."

Jack stares at his drink for a moment before holding it out for Gwen. "Drink, doc?"

"I'm serious about this, Jack."

"I can see that. You've got a real pickle up your ass, Gwen. Maybe it's time somebody pulled it out." He grabs her and yanks her out of the chair.

"Knock it off!"

"Don't be so stiff!"

"You're hurting me!"

"Believe me, Gwen, I'm not. Not yet, anyway." He slaps her across her face; blood runs from her nose. She slowly falls back into the chair. Intrigued by the blood, Jack wipes it off her face and smears it between his fingers. She cowers, dazed. "There are different degrees of hurt, Gwen. That was one level—this is another." Jack pulls her out of the chair and gets behind her, ripping her clothes off.

"What are you doing?!"

"I think it should be very clear what I'm doing." He continues tearing at her.

"What's wrong with you? Stop it!"

"Stop? I'm just getting started." But he suddenly stops. He feels an intense pain in his temples. He tries to continue with the rape but, in a moment of a Jekyll/Hyde struggle, he gasps in pain. He gets off her and staggers out of the house. Relieved, but confused, Gwen puts her skirt back in place.

Jack—he's Good Jack for this brief moment—staggers from the house. With a nod to Hamlet, he rubs his blood-stained hands together, frantically. He drops to his knees and submerges his hands in the pool, trying to wash his sins away. He becomes light-headed and falls in.

Hearing the splash, Gwen rushes out onto the deck and sees him floating in the water. "Oh my god! Jack! Jack!" She races down the stairs and jumps into the pool. She pulls his head out of the water. With great effort, she finally gets him out of the pool, gets on top of him, and performs CPR. Soon, Jack coughs and gasps for air. He struggles to clear his lungs—and his mind. Gwen is panic stricken. "That does it. I'm getting you out of this place. We're going home."

Jack sobs. "She's dead."

"What? Who's dead?"

"She's dead. It was an accident, but I let her drown. I wanted to help, but ..." Jack sobs and takes Kari's necklace out of his pocket. "I reached for her, she was falling … all I got was this."

"That's Kari's!" Gwen looks at her sobbing husband. For the first time in days, she feels pity for him and takes him in her arms.

Back in the bungalow, she sits naked on the steam-filled shower floor, knees pulled close to her chest and arms wrapped around her legs. She cries hysterically, staring straight ahead through the open door to the bedroom. Jack lies in bed, tossing and turning in the throes of another nightmare. She is almost numb to what she sees, but she continues to watch as he battles with his dream. It's a return to the nightmare in the field. Terrence Lee Horton, only a few feet away from Jack, cracks the neck of his female victim. Terrence turns to Jack; he has no eyes, just dark, empty sockets where eyes should be. Disturbed by this, Jack turns to the swollen and bloody victim. The lifeless face staring back at him is Gwen! He closes his eyes in horror, only to find when he opens them again that it is his own hands twisting the neck of his dead wife.

Chapter 33

At the old dock, a small shuttle boat pulls up and Sam, dressed for travel and carrying a small bag, steps off. His cell phone rings. "Hello? ... Gwen? ... I can hardly hear you. Hello?" Reacting to the dial tone, Sam hangs up, whispering to his phone as he slams it shut. "Kiss my ass."

Nearby, island residents Earl and Dell are on the deck of their boat and notice Sam's plight. Earl tries to help. "You don't get no signal out here. There's a pay phone on the newer dock by the resort—half mile that way."

"Actually, I just need directions. I'm looking for two friends of mine. One of them might be wearing dark glasses. They arrived a couple of days ago."

Earl takes a moment. "Oh, them two."

Dell nods. "She's a pretty one. Anyone would notice her."

“They’re stayin’ at the big bungalow, up there on that hill—the two-story one, past all them little bungalows.”

“Thank you.” Sam walks off in the direction Earl pointed. When he arrives at the bungalow, the front door is ajar. He knocks, then pokes his head in. “Hello? Gwen? Jack?” He hears opera music and follows the sound to the living room. Jack is sitting at the wet bar, slicing a lime with a large knife. The source of the music, the old record player, sits on the bar. Since Jack’s back is to the door, Sam isn’t sure if he heard him come in. He steps into the room. “Oh, there you are.”

Jack pauses from cutting the lime. His head raises slightly. A small smile cuts through his face. He doesn’t turn. “Hello, Sam. What a surprise.”

“Gwen didn’t tell you I was coming?”

“It must have slipped her mind—but how nice that you’re here. Join me for a drink—you’re a martini man as I recall.” He takes out a martini glass.

“It’s a little early for that.”

"Suit yourself." Jack picks up his own drink and turns to face Sam, who can't help but react to Jack's transformation—it is deranged, maniacal.

Sam feels uneasy, so he shifts his attention to the music playing. He picks up a record. "Opera? You?"

"Funny. Gwen said it that way, too … exactly that way. But you see, Sam—I've been expanding my interests, discovering new things." Jack stares at Sam, making him uncomfortable. "I didn't know you made house calls."

"Sure I do, Jack, for my very close friends."

Jack moves toward Sam. "Are we close friends, doc? Really close friends?"

Nervous, Sam looks around at his options. "Of course we are."

Jack moves in closer. "Here's what I think you are—an opportunist. I think you just want to be on the news. Well, Sam, it's your lucky day. I'm going to make it happen for you."

Jack holds up the knife. Sam runs for the door, but Jack steps in between, blocking his way. Sam spies another doorway at the other end of the room and bolts. It leads upstairs. Jack follows. At the bottom of the stairs, he smiles and calls out: "Think you're smart, don't you, Sam. Let's try this again—from the top." Jack slowly walks up the stairs.

Sam runs into a bedroom and grabs a lamp. Jack reaches the top of the stairs. A smile spreads across his face as he moves toward the bedroom.

Sam, breathing hard, listens for Jack. His hand tightens around the lamp; sweat beads on his forehead.

Jack, in the hallway, taunts Sam. "Doc, you shouldn't be afraid of me." He steps into the doorway. "You made me." Sam swings the lamp. Jack deflects the blow, knocking the lamp out of Sam's hands while backing him toward the wall. "So what do you have to say for yourself, 'friend?'" Sam starts to speak, but Jack covers his mouth with his hand. "I wouldn't believe anything you say, anyway." He moves closer with each word: "Only ... seeing ... is … BELIEVING!"

Chapter 34

Down by the dock, a crowd has gathered. Two locals haul Kari's body out of the water as the sheriff watches. A distraught and disoriented Ed Donalds stands under a tree, in shock. Dell and Earl are nearby, both clearly shaken. Gwen pushes through the crowd and stands next to Gretchen, who is fascinated with the event. She looks over to Gwen. "Sure has drawn a crowd. Just about everyone on the island is here. Pretty exciting, huh."

"What?"

"Shhh."

Sheriff Whitman walks over to Earl and Dell. "Tell me about it, boys."

"We was fishin' off the pier when Earl hooked what he thought was a sea lion, but it was that woman." He points to Kari's body.

Earl stammers: “I … I never expected nothin’ like this.”

The sheriff walks over to inspect the body. Deputy Harris pulls out the hook. “What do you think, Deputy?”

“I don’t see any trauma to the body or head. Just where Earl hooked her, Sheriff. Maybe it’s an accidental drowning?”

“I don’t know; I need to wait for the coroner’s report.”

Dell steps up and looks over the sheriff ’s shoulder. “Do you really think that’s all it was, Sheriff—just a drowning?”

“We don’t need to make more of this than it already is, Dell.” The sheriff uses his hand radio to contact his office. “Maggie?”

“Go ahead, Sheriff.”

“Tell Doc Craig I need him. Got a drowning. I’ll need a coroner’s report.”

“Roger, Sheriff.”

A call from the crowd of onlookers rings out. "Sheriff!" He looks over. When he sees it's Gretchen, he sighs and waits. "I just want to let you know ... they were both at the bar last night. No disrespect, but Ed was five sheets to the wind."

The sheriff dismisses her comment. "Thank you, Gretchen." He then walks over to Ed. "I sure am sorry about this, Ed. Is there anything you can tell me?"

"She was okay last I saw her ... said she was just going back on deck for a nightcap before coming to bed. Then I woke up to this ..."

In the crowd, Gretchen whispers to Gwen: "You know, your husband was there, too, at the bar. I ain't sayin' he had anything to do with this; I'm just sayin' he was there."

During this, Clarence pushes through the crowd. "Get out of the way, I need to talk to the sheriff! Sheriff, one of my guests just found a body on the trail off the North Shore." Then he sees Kari's body. "Oh my God."

Chapter 35

A shaken Bigler, holding his metal detector, is at the North Shore trail. Clarence stands by him as the sheriff kneels to look at the remains of a body in the unearthed grave. It is more skeleton than body. Gwen and a group of onlookers, including Gretchen, make their way onto the scene, clamoring among themselves and watching. The sheriff stands up and looks over to Bigler. "It's terrible. I don't know how I'll ever get this image out of my mind. I don't know how ..."

"Calm down, Mr. Bigler. Tell me how you found her."

"I started digging for metal and that's when I saw it—a gold band with a diamond. I went to pick it up and there was a stick through it, like a root. So I pulled on it—except it wasn't a root, it was a bone! Oh my God! I touched it! Don't you understand, I touched it!" He is overwhelmed. His wife, Mamie, moves close to comfort him.

Clarence leans in to the sheriff. "Hell, how we going to keep the lid on this one? Just about everyone on the island is here."

"We'll think of something, Clarence. We always do."

Gretchen, inching forward to where she is again standing next to Gwen, leans in and speaks quietly to her. "Betcha' that ain't the only one. Three women turned up missing here a few years ago. They never found a single one of the bodies ... until now, anyway. It was that killer—Terrence Lee Horton—the one they executed a while back."

"How do you know that?"

"'Cause I saw him. No one forgets that face, with those eyes ... kinda like your husband's."

"What are you talking about?"

"I'll show you."

They head to a dilapidated mobile home. The shrubbery is overgrown; piles of junk are stacked everywhere. Gretchen is clearly a pack rat. As they get to the door, Gretchen continues her story. "The sheriff and the people who run the resort, they don't believe it. They don't get it. Murder is good for business—always has been."

The inside of Gretchen's house is an eyesore. Newspapers are stacked to the ceiling. News clippings "decorate" the walls. All of the articles concern serial killings. Gretchen motions to them. "Of course, I didn't know who he was when he was here. That came later, after he was arrested and they started running his picture in the papers."

Gwen leans in to look at the clippings. It's a mess—everything is taped and tacked in no discernible order. Most contain mugshots of Horton intently staring into a camera. As Gwen looks at the pictures, Gretchen continues: "He killed 13 women that they know of. But you know there's got to be more. He always took a piece of them that represented their personality. I've made it my hobby to study men like him. A pretty girl can't be too careful. Here, this ought to interest you." She motions to a framed photo hanging on the wall. It shows a group of people, in the bar of the resort restaurant, smiling and toasting the camera. "This was taken the week those women vanished. Here's one ... and another ... and the third." Gretchen points to each of the three women, remembering them. Gwen notices a younger Gretchen in the photo. "There was a big party in the main ballroom. It was the Fourth of July. I was workin' that night—but then, I didn't end up dead, neither."

Gwen leans in and sees Horton among the revelers. She notices three framed pictures of Horton grouped together on the wall. Two are in black and white and do not reveal the color of his eyes; the last one, in color, does, but a newspaper article covers half of it. Gwen takes the picture off the wall and pulls the article away; now she can see the color of his eyes. A shiver runs down her spine. She drops the picture, breaking the glass. She is frozen in place.

Gretchen continues talking. "Of course, I brought this to the sheriff 's attention. But his job is to just make sure people keep coming to the island." Gwen's face reflects her moment of realization as she rushes out. Disappointed, Gretchen calls after her: “They’ll have to listen to me now. You can bet there’ll be plenty more excitement around here! You’ll see!”

Chapter 36

Gwen hurries back to the bungalow and rushes through the front door. She sees Sam's overnight bag on the floor and hears opera music playing. She hesitantly calls out: "Sam?"

Gwen steps into the room and sees the old Jack, friendly, happy, non-threatening. Sitting across from him, with his back toward Gwen, is Sam. In between them on the wet bar are two drinks; one is a martini. Seeing Gwen, Jack looks up and smiles. "Gwen, look who's here. It's our good friend, Sam."

Relieved, Gwen hurries further into the room. "Sam, I'm so happy to see ..." She freezes in her tracks. Sam is dead, propped up in the chair, with bloody holes where his eyes should be.

"We were just having a drink. Join us." Jack motions to the martini glass where Sam's eyeballs float, staring out at Gwen. She gasps. Jack smiles as she bolts out the door.

Gwen frantically runs toward the docks. There is no one in sight. A boat piloted by Earl and Dell passes. Gwen races to the edge of the dock and calls out. “Help! Please, help me!”

Earl cups his ear: “What?”

Gwen yells again: “I need your help! A man’s been killed!”

“I know, they found another body!”

Dell yells: “That’s three in one day!”

“I need help!”

Still not hearing, Earl points, calls out one last time: “Over there!”

Gwen looks around anxiously. She spots the pay phone and hurries to it. When she picks up the receiver, she sees that the wire has been cut. Desperate, she drops the receiver and runs back toward the dock. As she passes various boats, she looks around for anything that can protect her, going through several fishing tools until she decides on a fish gutting knife. “Hello! Please, anybody!" The area resembles a ghost town. She hurries further down the dock, then slows for a moment, thinking. "Gretchen!" She hurries off in the direction of Gretchen's house.

Clutching the knife, she runs up to Gretchen's door and bangs on it. "Gretchen, it's Gwen … Gwen Newman. Gretchen?" She tries the door; it's unlocked, so she goes in. Through the jungle of junk and stacks of newspapers, the wall of clippings is now orderly, not at all like it was earlier. The Horton clips are perfectly symmetrical, like a shrine. Numerous lit candles glow from the counter. The difference hits her: "Oh my God ... Jack's been here."

The front door closes. She spins with a gasp.

"Correction. Jack IS here."

Terrified, Gwen raises her knife. Jack holds up his even larger knife. He taunts her: "Mine's bigger than yours."

Without taking her eyes off of him, Gwen backs up. "You stay away from me, Jack!" He steps forward. "Don't you come near me. I'm not afraid to use this."

Jack smiles his evil smile. "You're afraid of everything, Gwen."

"Jack, please …"

"Listen to me, Gwen. Listen carefully ..."

Gwen gasps, then turns and runs deeper into the house. The "décor" gets worse the further in she goes. Clutter and filth add to the claustrophobia. She desperately searches for a way out. She finds a door; she fumbles with the handle and yanks it open, revealing a closet. Inside is Gretchen, dead, hanging on a hook. Her nose has been cut from her face. Gwen screams.

Jack appears in the hall, walking slowly, swinging his knife back and forth, and holding Gretchen's nose in his hand. "She was such a nosy woman. But not anymore!"

"Jack, please, don't ..."

"I've always been very particular about which body part I would collect. It was easy with her. It was easy with Kari. But I'm torn with you … you're a complicated woman, Gwendolyn. Which do I take … your heart ... or your brain?"

"Stay away, Jack! I swear I'll use this knife!"

"Let's not waste my time. I know what I want now. You're clever, Gwen. I want your brain."

Gwen spies the house's back door; she swings it open but stays inside, hiding behind a chair.

Jack continues down the hallway and notices the open door. "Oh, Gwen, you ARE a clever one." He walks outside and looks around. When he doesn't see Gwen, he goes back inside the trailer.

Gwen takes this opportunity to run out of the house. She frantically crawls through slime and mud, still wielding the knife. Caked with dirt, she presses her back against the house, searching for a direction to run. Seconds later, the front door swings open. Jack steps out and looks around again. He descends the steps, leans down and looks under the house. Gwen's muddy footprints lead into the grass. He smiles. "You can't get away, Gwen—no one's going to help you. They're all on the other side of the island—digging up bodies. It's just you and me, baby. The honeymoon's over." Gripping his knife, he walks off in the direction of Gwen's footprints.

Gwen lies on the floor of a small wooden boat near Gretchen's house, watching as Jack disappears into the foliage. She rolls on her back, relieved—for the moment. After what seems like an eternity, and now under the cover of darkness, she looks in all directions and then slips out of the boat, her clothes covered in dried dirt. She creeps into the woods, in the same direction Jack went, toward the resort. Thunder rumbles; lightning cracks; the sky gets darker as she runs. She falls and twists her ankle, but she gets up and continues to limp toward safety. Jack sees her and goes after her. Gwen sees Witt locking up the restaurant. She runs to him for help, but he doesn't understand what she is saying since she is hysterical. Jack comes around the corner, brandishing his huge knife. Witt puts up his hand to protect himself; Jack drives the knife through Witt's hand. He bends over in pain. Jack then stabs Witt in his stomach; he falls down dead. Gwen, not knowing what to do, runs off into the darkness.

Chapter 37

In his yacht, Ed is sitting on the couch drinking when the phone rings. It's a friend who has heard the news. "I leave tomorrow, got to make arrangements. Thank you. Thank you very much." He lays down his phone by his gun. His glass empty, he walks over to the bar, unscrews a bottle and pours himself a drink. He hears something on the roof; when he looks behind him, he sees Jack, holding his gun. "Where in the hell did you come from?"

Jack just looks at him. "Do you remember me?"

"Yes, you're the one who liked my wife's necklace."

"Yes, the necklace. You have very good taste."

Ed slowly sits back down on the couch; Jack sits across from him. "Why are you here, Jack?"

"Some unfinished business."

"You like my wife's necklace, you like my gun, you like my yacht. What else do you want?"

"Your life." Jack points the gun at Ed.

Ed's mouth quivers as they stare at each other. "Well, it's been a good one." He raises his drink as to do a toast. "To love."

Jack toasts "To love" and shoots him.

Chapter 38

The fog rolls in; Gwen, on the run again, sees lights are on in a few of the boats. She hurries toward them, hoping to find someone. She runs to the first boat. "Hello! Somebody, please help me!" No response. She runs over a small bridge and comes face to face with the sheriff. She gasps, but is quickly relieved to see that it is the sheriff and not Jack. "Oh, Sheriff ..."

The sheriff sees the knife in her hand and steps back. "I've been looking for you—you and that husband of yours. I have a few questions for him about the Congressman's wife ..."

"He's not my husband. I know it sounds crazy, but he's somebody else ... he's that killer, Terrence Lee Horton ..."

A dark look crosses the sheriff 's face. "I saw you talking to Gretchen; did she put this nonsense in your head?"

“She’s dead! He killed her. She’s back at her house. He killed a man, too … a doctor ... Sam Rieland ... his body’s in the house where we are staying.”

“I’ve been to that house, lookin’ for you and your husband. There ain’t no body there.”

“It was! Jack cut his eyes out and put them in a martini glass.” Gwen stops, realizing how crazy she must sound.

The sheriff holds out his hand. “Give me the knife.”

Gwen takes a step back. “No.”

“Lady, I don’t know what’s going on in your head. I don’t know what’s going on in your marriage, either. But we’ve had one hell of a day out here, and I’m not much in the mood for any more of this.”

Jack suddenly appears behind the sheriff. He reaches around and slashes his throat. The sheriff ’s look of skepticism changes to one of horror and surprise. He clutches his throat, trying to speak. Gwen watches, horrified, as blood gushes from between his fingers. The sheriff drops to the ground, leaving her face to face with Jack. She runs down into an old dock that looks as though at any moment it could give way into the water. Jack is right behind her; she has no place to run.

"Here we are, Gwen, the way you wanted it—just you and me, baby."

Gwen shakes her head; Jack backs her against a wall. She swipes the knife, trying to cut him, but he effortlessly knocks it out of her hand, keeping the bigger knife for himself. "You seem to be confused about something, Gwen. You told the sheriff I'm Horton. I'm not Horton—I'm Jack." Gwen tries to run past him, but he flings her back against the railing. "You know I've always been fascinated with evil. I discuss it with my students—what makes a person do horrible, dark things?" Gwen again tries to get away; Jack again shoves her back. "Somehow, since the operation, I've been ... enlightened. I can see what Horton saw, those horrible things he did. I suppose his eyes have helped me understand ... evil." Gwen lashes out, swinging at him. He throws her to the dock, then straddles her, pinning her arms down. "I want to put this thought in your head before I take your brain. It'll make it all the more special. I've learned from Horton that we all have evil within, all of us—it's inside you, too."

"No it's not!"

"Yes, Gwen, even you. But as we're civilized, social creatures, we've been taught to control our primal instincts. We just can't go around bashing each other's heads in, now can we?"

Gwen sobs. "Jack, please ..."

"Listen to me, this is important. When we put restraints on our own personal evil, we're not truly free. And if we are not truly free, we are not truly alive." Gwen tries to shift away, whimpering. Jack turns her face to his. "For those who suppress evil, the only freedom they have to look forward to in life ... is in death." He leans in closer. "My gift to you, darling, is your freedom."

Jack presses his knife against Gwen's forehead. Terrified, she struggles and manages to fold her leg between herself and Jack. With her foot she throws him back, impaling him on a pole. She is horrified.

Jack, still Evil Jack, tries to move, but he is paralyzed below the arms. He looks down at the bloodied shaft of wood protruding from his chest. "Oh ..." He looks at Gwen. The evil seems to drain from his face, returning him to Good Jack. Gwen takes an apprehensive step toward him. "Gwen ... thank God you're safe."

As Gwen stares at Jack, her eyes well with tears. "You're free now, baby."

Jack slowly reaches out to touch her face like he did with the sculpture of her not that long ago. "When you're upset ... this muscle tightens more ... than the other..." As his words trail off, Gwen puts both hands on his face as she struggles to get the slightest word out, her face filled with tears. Jack smiles, holding his gaze until his eyes slowly go dead. Emotionally drained, Gwen slides her trembling body down to her knees. She tries to soothe herself by rocking.

Morning comes. Gwen, still on the old dock, stares at the calm water. A beam of early sunlight finally breaks her daydreaming. Several sheriff deputies investigate the murder scene; one of the officers walks over to Gwen and wraps a blanket around her. After a moment, she returns her gaze to the water.

Chapter 39

“So we can see that the nature of evil is not something as clearly defined as we might think. For some, evil will be an abstract battle, a notional debate about the actions of man ...” It’s been eight months, and a very pregnant Gwen lectures a class. “So, consider this: is evil born, bred, nurtured or simply the work of the ‘devil?’” She seems to speak as much to herself as to the class. “For others, it is more personal. Evil is ... a very personal thing. A very real thing.” A bright red apple sits on her desk by a wedding picture of her and Jack. She stares at the picture as the students exit the classroom.

Six months later, she sits on a bench enjoying a beautiful day at the neighborhood park. A lot of people are in the park having fun, walking their dogs, throwing frisbees. A baby begins to cry. “Hush, hush, little one. Daddy and I love you. He’s watching ...” The baby stops crying and looks up at her with his beautiful blue eyes. “He’s watching, he’s always watching.”

The End

Mamie Jean Calvert is a distinguished professional in the realm of entertainment, boasting a multifaceted career as an award-winning screenwriter, accomplished author, seasoned movie producer, adept director, and talented actress who has appeared in several movies. Her keen understanding of the filmmaking process and her ability to breathe life into characters on both sides of the camera have solidified her reputation as a versatile and accomplished professional.

With a passion for crafting compelling narratives, Mamie Jean has earned recognition for her outstanding screenwriting, receiving prestigious awards that underscore her dedication to the art of storytelling. She graduated from the Hollywood Film Institute and earned enough TV show credits to give her a seat in the Producers Guild.

As an author, she has seamlessly transitioned her storytelling expertise to the literary world, captivating readers with her evocative prose and imaginative narratives. An accomplished author, Mamie Jean is now publishing her fifth book.

Mamie Jean Calvert, along with her loving husband Robert, calls Elk Grove, California, home, finding inspiration in the serene surroundings. Her commitment to the craft, coupled with her diverse skill set, continues to leave an indelible mark on the world of entertainment, making her a respected figure in the industry, doing what she loves.

To Judy Nessen, my exceptional editor and a luminary in the world of Microsoft technical editing. With an illustrious career spanning Internet Explorer and the Developer Network, Judy's expertise has touched diverse realms. Her freelance editing ventures, from scrutinizing medical studies on radiation effects to refining historical fiction, a guidebook for nannies, and TV series scripts, showcase her versatile talents. Judy's passion lies in proofreading, meticulously catching overlooked errors. From her early days in radio broadcasting, spanning Los Angeles to New York City, to her influential roles at ON TV, SelectTV, and the Ingle Company, Judy’s journey is marked by a commitment to excellence. Collaborating with Mamie Jean, she contributed to numerous movie scripts and books, even earning acclaim as the script supervisor for the award-winning film *In the Eyes of a Killer/Blindsided.* Born and raised in Spokane, Washington, Judy continues to reside on her childhood acreage, surrounded by the love of her two sons, three grandsons, and one granddaughter. This dedication is a tribute to my long-time friend for decades, a remarkable editor, and an inspiring individual whose impact resonates far beyond the written word.

PART 2

In the Eyes of a Killer

How it Originated

Script

The Origin of In the Eyes of a Killer

How did *In the Eyes of a Killer* come to be? I penned the original script, which evolved into a thrilling movie, and has now been transformed into a book. The inspiration for the story struck me when a girlfriend, the sole survivor among eight liver transplant recipients, shared her experiences. Witnessing the changes in her lifestyle—her taste in music, dietary preferences, and the unexpected growth of curly black hair beneath her original dark blonde locks—I became intrigued. She knew only that her transplanted organ came from a 21-year-old man who had tragically lost his life in a motorcycle accident.

This script wasn't my first attempt, but it was the one I took most seriously. I began by crafting a backstory for the main character, Terrence Lee Horton, and delving into the lives of his parents, Jeff and Helen Horton. Their tumultuous marriage ended when Helen discovered Jeff's infidelity with her sister. Pregnant at the time, she gave birth to Terrence Lee.

After he was born, she couldn't bear to look at his striking resemblance to his unfaithful father. Consequently, Terrence was raised by his grandmother on a small island in the California Delta, enduring a lonely and harsh childhood. Over the years, he became a serial killer. His mother became an alcoholic and died young, and his father was killed in a car accident.

Fueled by my passion for the project and with the support of my husband, we embarked on preproduction, investing our entire savings. Fortunately, I met Karla through a friend, Laurie, who brought invaluable knowledge to the project. The journey began, but not without its challenges.

Securing a location for the shoot was a crucial step. During a business meeting, I approached Witt Whitman, suggesting his resort as an ideal setting. To my delight, he offered his resort, and the dream started to materialize. Seven months of intensive preproduction followed; with the initial working title *In the Eyes of the Beholder* eventually changing to *In the Eyes of a Killer* due to misconceptions about possible religious undertones. The actual filming spanned 15 days, made possible also by the support of angel investors who believed in the project. The movie won 12 film awards. It sold in many foreign countries and later was picked up by Monarch Films.

I express my heartfelt gratitude to the executive producers and everyone involved. The completion of this film was truly a collaborative effort. You really do need a village to shoot a movie.

Thank you all from the bottom of my heart.

Mamie Jean

PART 3

IN THE EYES OF A KILLER

FADE IN:

1. INT. PRISON CORRIDOR - NIGHT 1

Three men walk down a long, dark corridor. In the middle is prisoner TERRENCE LEE HORTON, a man in his mid-forties with one striking feature. His eyes. One dark brown, the other, piercing blue - together, create a very disturbing presencc. Flanking Horton are TWO PRISON GUARDS.

2. INT. PRISON EXECUTION ROOM - MOMENTS LATER 2

Horton and the Prison Guards enter. A METAL TABLE sits in

the center. The WARDEN and PRISON DOCTOR stand to the side. As the Guards lead Horton to the table, he stops in front of the GLASS MIRROR and stares, clearly aware there are people on the other side.

ANGLE - VIEWING ROOM

As Horton looks into the room we see what he cannot: several of the VICTIMS' FAMILY MEMBERS, PRESS and PRISON OFFICIALS,

waiting, watching. The witnesses grow increasingly uncomfortable with Horton's evil stare. A SKETCH ARTIST works on the scene on his artist's pad.

ANGLE - EXECUTION ROOM

Horton continues to glare into the glass, even when the Warden motions for the Guards to move him into position. As the Doctor and Guards prepare the table:

WARDEN

Terrence Lee Horton, you have been duly convicted by the state of California for the rape and murder of Ann Miller ...

C.U. Of Horton's face. His chilling expression does not change. (INTERCUT with PICTURES of the murdered women and the faces of the victims' families as they react to the calling out of the names).

WARDEN (cont'd)

- Carrie McCall ... Joanne Wilson, Chelsea Joy...and Laura Jean.

Judgement has bccn passed that you be executed for these crimes. Do you have any final words?

Horton continues to stare through the glass.

HORTON

There are more - And I'll take them to my grave.

The Warden signals to Guard #1 to put the prisoner in place. As Horton lays on the table, we BEGIN A SERIES OF CLOSE UPS; ARMS STRAPPED TO A TABLE, ANKLE CHAINS LOCKED IN PLACE, THE

ARM TATTOOS OF HORTON. As the final strap is secured, the Doctor moves to the prisoner and swabs his arm with ALCOHOL, and then the CANULA is inserted.

The Warden checks his POCKET WATCH. ANGLE - VIEWING ROOM

The witnesses anxiously wait. The wall clock strikes 12. ANGLE - EXECUTION ROOM

The Warden confirms the time on his watch, and nods. A machine O.S. purrs to life. Solution runs through the clear tubes into Horton's arm. He begins to lose unconsciousness, however, continues his look of controlled insanity and hatred until his breathing slows and finally stops. All that can be heard is FLAT LINE TONE.

ANGLE - VIEWING ROOM

The families watch. One person quietly sobs. The others remain quiet and still.

ANGLE - EXECUTION ROOM

The Doctor listens to Horton's heart with a STETHOSCOPE and nods to the Warden. The Warden motions for the Guards to take the body away. Guard #1 joins in to assist Guard #2 with Horton.

GUARD #1

(whispering)

I don't get this guy - someone like him donating organs?

GUARD #2

The asshole probably thinks he'll live forever.

WARDEN

(overhearing) Gentlemen.

The Guards react to the "scolding" and quicken their pace. On the way out Guard #1 closes the BLACK VIEWING ROOM CURTAIN.

CUT TO:

3. INT. UNIVERSITY LECTURE HALL - DAY 3

Horrific images of murders are projected onto a screen via POWER POINT - intercut with the following:

JACK'S VOICE (O.C.)

What is evil? How is it created? And why does it exist?

WIDER ANGLE reveals the dimly lit LECTURE HALL is filled with attentive students. The speaker, a man in a DARK SUIT, controls the show with a REMOTE. He addresses the class.

JACK

In order to understand evil, many cultures attribute it to inherent social conditions, a person's upbringing. Others blame genetics - claiming we are born with it. Most religions, however, prefer to ascribe evil to a presence, a being. You've all heard it ...

"the devil made me do it."

Jack CLICKS - a gory murder scene covers the screen.

JACK (cont'd)

Son of Sam, Charles Manson, take your pick. Right now, today, for every 100 people in America, one is a clinical psychopath.

STUDENT

That's a pretty pessimistic opinion of society, don't you think, Professor?

JACK

You don't see the world I do.

The class chuckles, uneasily. We will soon know why.

JACK (cont'd) Besides, it's not opinion, it's fact. Psychopaths in general harbor immense anger.

(MORE)

JACK (cont'd)

The majority of psychopaths find pleasure enough in just fantasizing the sufferings of those who annoy them. Those are the ones who walk amongst us, unnoticed.

The class shuffles uncomfortably as faces of normal everyday people flash on the screen.

JACK (cont'd)

Studies indicate that they simply do not feel nor can they understand the sufferings of others.

Jack's WATCH BEEPS.

JACK (cont'd)

When we meet again, we will discuss

... the devil.

The students collect their books and quickly file out.

Jack moves to his desk. He arranges the items on his desk without looking, then opens a BOOK. He seems to be reading in the dark as he runs his hands over the pages. CLICK. The OVERHEAD LIGHT goes on. Reacting to the sound, not the light, Jack cocks his head.

GWEN (O.S.)

"Discuss the devil"? - You trying to make education fun, Professor?

GWEN, an attractive and professional woman in her early thirties, steps into the room.

JACK

Well ... no one fell asleep. How do you keep them awake in your Psychology classes?

GWEN

I talk about penis envy.

Jack smiles.

GWEN (cont'd)

Come on, let's go for a walk.

Jack reaches for a WHITE CANE. Gwen moves close, Jack takes her arm.

JACK

After you, Professor. We'll bump into less walls that way.

4. EXT. CAMPUS - DAY 4

Fall weather. Students mill around the campus. Gwen and Jack, in the middle of their stroll, walk arm in arm. Jack carries his white cane.

GWEN

Did our friend the good Doctor call?

JACK

He calls me every day.

GWEN

(pausing for a moment thinking Jack will continue)

Sam just wants us to be happy.

JACK

We <u>are</u> happy.

GWEN

Okay.

(with a smile)

Happier.

JACK

(intentionally changing the subject)

My favorite time of the year. Seeing the leafs turn color - such beauty.

GWEN

(playing along) And you see this?

JACK

In a way.

GWEN

I'm late for class sweetie, see you tonight?

JACK

I hope so.

Gwen kisses Jack and walks off. Jack smiles, then, using his white cane, starts back toward the building.

CUT TO:

5. EXT. SALLY'S HOUSE-PATIO-DAY 5

GWEN and friend SALLY sit outside DRINKING COFEE. Gwen chews on a CANDY BAR.

SALLY

How did you survive before you met Jack? Candy bars?

(pause)

You’re lucky you’re marrying a man who can cook - and lucky he’s blind.

Lucky?

GWEN

SALLY

All I know is, if I had a blind guy, I’d want to keep him that way. I’d save a fortune on cosmetics.

(takes a sip of coffee) So have you decided where the wedding’s going to be?

GWEN

Since neither of us have family in the area, Jack was thinking Vegas - He’s somehow got it in his head he wants to be married by Elvis.

SALLY

An Elvis impersonator?! Oh my god, are you serious?

GWEN

Jack is.

Gwen takes a sip of coffee.

SALLY

Elvis? I would just scream!

CUT TO:

6. B-MOVIE ON TV SCREEN - EXT. TREE LINED AREA-NIGHT 6

A SCREAM. A FRIGHTENED WOMAN runs through a dark corn field, terrified, her breathing rapid, eyes darting. She turns, CAMERA SHIFTS and she is nose to nose with the face of terror:

A HANDSOME PSYCHOPATH, holds a BUTCHER KNIFE.

Frightened Woman GASPS - but is too terrified to move.

Frightened Woman finally turns and runs. The killer bellows sadistic laughter.

FRESH ANGLE - Frightened Woman races faster through field trying to escape. She can't.

She tries to run a different direction, revealing gthe killer right in front of her.

Paralyzed by fear, the woman is backed into a tree. The psychopath raises his bloody implements of murder and mayhem. Terrified, Frightened Woman SCREAMS.

CUT TO:

7. INT. HOUSE - KITCHEN - EVENING 7

PAN to reveal a SMALL TV SET on kitchen counter. The image of mayhem from the previous scene now picks up on the TV

screen - we are watching a slasher movie. Jack laughs at the ridiculous sounds comings from the television set.

WIDER ANGLE reveals:

Everything is neat and orderly where Jack prepares dinner.

As the screaming and SUSPENSEFUL MUSIC continues from the TV, he reaches into a cabinet and takes out a LARGE POT. At the sink, he runs water, filling the pot and testing the level with his finger, then sets it on the stove and turns on the gas. He finds the SPAGHETTI and SAUCE INGREDIENTS.

8. INT. DINING ROOM - EVENING 8

Gwen enters, carrying an armful of GROCERIES and FLOWERS. She smiles, seeing the perfectly SET TABLE, then reacts to the filtered sounds of screaming. The smile fades, and she exits to:

9. INT. KITCHEN - CONTINUOUS 9

Gwen enters and sets the groceries on the counter. She

kisses Jack's cheek. (On TV, the killer has caught up to his victim and slashes away).

GWEN

How can you stand watching this?

JACK

Actually, it's radio to me. I'm trying to prepare for my next lecture - Satan.

GWEN

Oh - kay ... Well, prepare it some other time. Not before dinner.

Gwen turns off the TV.

JACK

(teasing)

You know, for a psych teacher you really need to get over your fear of maniacs with meat cleavers - they're out there.

GWEN

Yeah, well as long as they *stay*

"out there" - *way* out there. (changing subject)

Let's talk about something else.

Anything else. Smells good.

Gwen uses a spoon to stir the sauce and lift some up to her face for a sniff and little taste. She returns the spoon to the counter, an inch from where she picked it up. Jack seems to sense this, and moves the spoon back to where it started. He smiles at Gwen.

GWEN (cont'd) Sorry, chef.

Jack's hands search the counter, making sure everything is in its proper place.

JACK

It's the only way I can find things.

GWEN

I'll get out of your way. (sacastically)

It's a shame, though. You know I'd love to help. I'm a real whiz in the kitchen.

Gwen heads for the door, happy to be escaping kitchen chores. The moment she is gone, Jack switched the TV back on (for more screaming from Frightened Woman).

10. INT. DINING ROOM - NIGHT 10

The REMAINS OF DINNER cover the table. CANDLES are burnt low. Both Gwen and Jack look full and satisfied. Gwen stares at the empty dishes on the table.

GWEN

I can't believe how good that was.

JACK

(beat) Close your eyes.

GWEN

Why?

JACK

Just close them.

Gwen closes her eyes. After a few moments she begins to sneak a peek.

JACK (cont'd) No peeking.

Caught, Gwen shuts them.

Jack goes to the CHINA CUPBOARD and opens a door, revealing a CLOTH COVERED OBJECT. He places it in front of Gwen.

JACK (cont'd) Open your eyes.

Eyes open.

Jack pulls the cloth off, revealing a near perfect CLAY FACIAL EXPRESSION of Gwen. The detail is uncannily precise.

GWEN

Oh my God - it's me. (to Jack)

Where did you did get this?

JACK

Actually ... I made it.

GWEN

(startled)

You?! ... but ... how? I

mean...you can't...

JACK

I can see you.

Jack touches the lines on Gwen's forehead.

JACK (cont'd) Just as I thought. I see skepticism.

Gwen forces the lines to go away. Jack grins.

Still touching Gwen's forehead with one hand, Jack touches the forehead of the facial expression with the other, tracing it with his fingers.

JACK (cont'd) See? I know your face.

Jack traces the real Gwen and the plaster Gwen, simultaneously, reaching her smiling lips.

JACK (cont'd)

There. The same curve, with just the slightest dimple here.

GWEN

Okay, I get ...

JACK

(interrupting) Shhh ...

Jack lightly closes Gwen's lips with his fingers. He traces her neck as he follows along on the plaster one.

JACK (cont'd)

When you get upset, this muscle tightens more than the other one. Upset ... or ... aroused.

Gwen tries to speak, but again:

JACK (cont'd)

Shhh ...

Jack traces down to Gwen's breasts. Gwen smiles.

11. INT. BEDROOM - EVENING/NIGHT 11

AN ELVIS SOUNDING BALLAD softly plays in the background. CLOSE UP Jack and Gwen kiss as light of a full moon shines

through the window and envelopes them in a soft glow. Jack moves across Gwen's semi-naked body, kissing, caressing, and exploring as only a blind man can.

JACK

My next sculpture will be a full body - from your lips ... to your breasts ... to your stomach... to your toes.

Gwen giggles as Jack reaches her toes.

JACK (cont'd)

I knew you were the one for me the first time we did this.

GWEN

(a slight chuckle) Made love?

JACK

No. When we touched. The day we met.

GWEN

(remembering)

I dropped my books when I bumped into you. I was so embarrassed!

JACK

When I went to pick them up, your arm brushed against my cheek. I knew instantly we'd be sharing our lives together.

GWEN

So, you're saying...it was love at first "sight?"

JACK

Better.

Gwen smiles, Jack senses her skepticism again and takes a SCARF from the night table and blindfolds Gwen.

JACK (cont'd) Now. Tell me what you feel.

GWEN

What's this?

JACK

Just put it on. I'm going to show you how *I* see *you.*

Gwen plays along and buts the scarf over her eyes. Gwen touches Jacks face.

GWEN

Okay. I feel you.

Gwen moves her hands on Jacks chest. When she reaches his chest, she puts her ear to it and listens.

GWEN (cont'd) I hear the sound of life.

Gwen kisses Jack's hand.

GWEN (cont'd) I can taste you.

Jack guides Gwen's lips to his. They kiss as Jack lays Gwen down out of frame.

GWEN (O.S.) (cont'd)

And what's this? I see someone who's very happy to "see" me.

Elvis sounding ballad swells as we...

CUT TO:

12. INT. PRIVATE DOCTOR'S OFFICE - NEXT DAY 12

DR. SAM RIELAND sits at his desk. Gwen sits across from him, as Jack paces in front of an EYE DIAGRAM

SAM

If I didn't know you better, Jack, I'd think you were having second thoughts about this surgery.

(off Jack's silence)

When I called this morning to tell you we'd found a donor, you said you had to check your calender.

JACK

I'm here, aren't I? (touches Gwen)

We're here.

GWEN

All he talks about is how much he wants this, Sam. It's just ...

(she looks at Jack pacing)

... well ...

SAM

Sometimes getting what we want can be frightening?

JACK

I'm not frightened. (then, begrudgingly)

Tell me about the donor.

SAM

You can relax. He was about your age with 20/20 vision. And healthy.

JACK

Apparently not so healthy - he's dead, isn't he?

SAM

The eyes are healthy. That's all we're concerned about.

Sam looks at his desk calender.

SAM (cont'd)

We can schedule the surgery for tomorrow.

JACK

Oh ... that soon?

SAM

Jack, we've talked about this. When eyes become available we've got to move quickly.

JACK

It's just hard to imagine this is going to work.

SAM

This *will* work, Jack. I wouldn't recommend it otherwise. After six years of testing, we're convinced we can move on to the next level.

JACK

Yeah, but those test were done on rats. And what about all the research finding cellular memory in heart and other organ donors?

GWEN

Cellular memory?

SAM

It's not what it sounds like. You're not picking up the memories of the donor - it means that the cell is remembering functioning in the body. That's all.

JACK

I've read stuff, Sam, there's other theories ...

SAM

All bogus. You want facts? Donor recipients tend to live long, rich lives without setbacks. This is a real chance for you, Jack.

Jack turns away as Gwen and Sam exchange frustrated looks.

SAM (cont'd)

Jack...

JACK

I just don't know.

SAM

Jack, this isn't something new. We've talked about this for months. You even knew I was inviting the press here today. They're outside - <u>now</u> - waiting to meet you - waiting for the big announcement.

Jack remains silent, his back to them. Gwen moves to Jack. She touches his face.

GWEN

(softly)

Sweetheart, isn't this what you always hoped for? With this you have a chance to finally have your sight again.

Jack looks queasy.

JACK

I need to get some air. Jack exits. Gwen looks troubled.

GWEN

He'll be okay - it's just pre-op jitters. Everyone gets them.

Right?

SAM

Gwen, it could be another six months or a year, or longer, before we get another match. I thought we were all in agreement. If the opportunity came up we would move on it. Well, it's here - now.

Gwen moves to the window, guarding the concern on her face.

GWEN

How do we know the diabetes won't cause a problem with the new eyes?

SAM

His diabetes has been under control for years. The damage was done before he'd been diagnosed properly.

Gwen instantly reacts to something she sees through the window.

GWEN

Oh my god!

13. EXT. MEDICAL CENTER/ACCESS ROAD - DAY 13

A speeding CAR SWERVES and HONKS, nearly clipping Jack as he crosses the road.

REVERSE ANGLE

We see what Jack is trying to escape: A GROUP OF REPORTERS, at least one with a VIDEO CAMERA, have pursued Jack to the edge of the street.

REPORTER (CALLS OUT)

Hey, take it easy buddy, we just want to ask you a couple of questions.

VARIOUS ANGLES

JACK

I've got nothing to say.

Gwen hurries from the Medical Building and pushes her way through the Reporters.

GWEN

Jack, it's okay - I'm coming to get you.

As Gwen steps off the curb, a Reporter distracts her.

REPORTER

Hey, are you his wife? Is he the guy who's going to have the transplant? We just need a sound byte for the news.

GWEN

Leave him alone. He's not ready...

Gwen reacts to the sound of SCREECHING BRAKES - she spins to see a car stop just short of her.

The News Men do nothing to help, but they roll their cameras.

DRIVER (YELLS)

What are you - blind?!

Gwen, flustered, makes her way to the other side of the road, joining Jack.

Concerned, Jack takes Gwen's hands.

JACK

Are you okay?

GWEN

I fine, what were you trying to do?

A brief moment - both are relived to be alive and together.

JACK

(looking back at the group of reporters)

Let's go home.

CUT TO:

14. INT. KITCHEN - NIGHT 14

Jack expertly chops vegetables for dinner, his back to Gwen.

Gwen gently moves the facial impression Jack made of her and sits down. She studies the detail.

GWEN

I feel like I'm looking in a mirror

- this is really amazing, Jack. (turns to Jack)

Imagine what you'll be able to do once you can see.

Gwen, reacting to Jack's silence, goes to him and looks closely at his face.

CHOP CHOP CHOP.

Gwen waits. Jack senses that she is there - and speaks:

JACK

You know, I do okay. As a matter of fact, I think I'm happier now then when I could see. I don't take anything for granted anymore. I must be crazy to even be considering doing this.

Gwen strokes Jack's hair.

GWEN

You'll be okay.

JACK

(agitated)

I can get to work on the bus. I can support myself. I can cook. I can clean. I shouldn't have to prove that to you.

GWEN

Jack, you don't...

JACK

(interrupting)

Just in this room alone - I can find things faster than anyone with eyes.

Jack grabs his white cane and starts pointing with it.

JACK (cont'd) There's the stove.

(points)

The medium button is here.

Jack punches the medium button with his cane, on and off.

JACK (cont'd) The sink is here.

(points)

Hot.

(points)

Cold.

(points)

The toaster is here.

Jack swings the cane around and knocks the facial impression of Gwen over. It falls to the floor and shatters.

Jack is silent, then drops to his knees and frantically tries to pick up the pieces.

GWEN

Jack, it's okay. Jack cuts himself - reacts.

Gwen grabs a wet cloth, cleans Jack's cut hand and tries to sooth him.

GWEN (cont'd)

Honey, it's okay. You can make another one.

JACK

(realization) No ... No, I can't.

(then)

I can't protect you.

Jack tries to reach for more pieces. Gwen pulls his hand back.

GWEN

(RE: the broken bust) What? It's not me, Jack.

JACK

Today this could have been you - because of me. You look out for me, Gwen - I need ... I <u>want</u> to look out for you.

Push in on the broken pieces of sculpture as we hold on an a CLAY EYE SOCKET WITH A DROP OF BLOOD.

DISSOLVE TO:

15. INT. OPERATING ROOM - DAY 15

Sam and an ASSISTANT, along with an OPERATING ROOM STAFF,

conduct the eye transplant surgery on Jack as a CAMERA CREW documents the procedure. Sam seems to relish the attention. A montage follows:

A) Jack prepped for surgery.

B) A doctor sets up a camera & monitor.

C) Gwen in the waiting room, watching the clock, pacing.

D) A set of clamps keep Jack's eyes wide open.

E) Sam removing Jack's original eyes.

F) An assistant carting in a SOLUTION FILLED JAR with a PAIR OF EYES inside. One is blue. One is brown.

Sam picks up the jar and examines them.

SAM

(whispering to Assistant) They're two different colors.

ASSISTANT

(whispering back)

I know. I checked, they're from the same donor.

SAM

Are we going to have a legal problem with this?

ASSISTANT

His form stated eye color didn't matter.

Sam looks down at Jack, who is "out."

SAM

At least he'll see.

G) As Sam sets in the new eyes.

E.) Jack sleeping after surgery:

DISSOLVE TO:

16. INT. RECOVERY ROOM - DAY 16

Jack lays in bed. His head and eyes are bandaged.

SAM

(O.C.)

Jack?

Sam moves to Jack's bedside and touches him gently on the shoulder.

SAM (cont'd) Jack, you awake?

JACK

(drowsy) Yeah.

SAM

How do you feel?

JACK

Head ... hurts.

SAM

I'd be concerned if it didn't.

JACK

So - how'd it go?

SAM

I think it went very well. (beat)

I need to tell you something, Jack. We never talked about the color of the eyes.

JACK

It didn't matter - I had Gwen note that on the form.

SAM

We know that, that's why we proceeded with the surgery. But

... you have a very special pair of eyes. It's almost like you have two sets, actually.

JACK

(a joke)

You put four eyes in me?

SAM

We're going to get enough attention as it is. But they are unique.

You've got a blue and a brown one.

JACK

Well ... that'll be interesting when I get my driver's license.

SAM

At least you'll *have* a drivers license.

Sam pats Jack's leg.

SAM (cont'd) Time to meet the press.

Sam moves to the door. Before opening it:

SAM (cont'd)

Don't mention the headache. We're not getting paid to sell aspirin.

Sam opens the door.

SAM (cont'd) Alright, gentlemen, come in and meet the future.

A Camera Crew and/or Reporters enter (with appropriate ad- libs). After a few questions Jack seems to become overwhelmed. Sam notices Gwen enter the doorway and decides to end the interview.

SAM (cont'd)

Alright, everybody, there will be plenty of time to meet our famous patient later. Let's give him some breathing room.

As the press exits Gwen enters the room and sits next to Jack as he falls asleep.

C.U. Of Jack's bandaged eyes.

CUT TO:

17. INT. HOSPITAL ROOM - DAY 17

Sam cuts the bandages off Jack's head. Jack keeps his eyes closed for a few moments before slowly opening them.

We see what Jack sees, a blur of colors and shapes. Gwen reacts to the two different colored eyes.

As Jack makes an effort to force open his eyes, he instantly closes them again, covering them with his hands.

The NURSE hands Sam a bottle of SOLUTION. He opens one of Jack's eyes and applies the solution.

SAM

Alright, Jack, let's try again. Slowly this time.

C.U. of Jack's eyes as he tries again, blinking. We see Jack's P.O.V. of shapes and forms of the people. The CAMERA BRINGS THEM INTO FOCUS.

JACK

My God, it worked ... I can see.

Jack takes in the sights of the room. Gwen, apprehensive, inches closer.

JACK (cont'd)

I see you.

(smiles)

I can *really* see you.

Gwen rushes to Jack and kisses him, as both share the joyful moment.

JACK (cont'd) (touching her face)

I memorized you face, but, you're more beautiful than I even imagined.

(beat)

What about me? How do I look? Gwen covers the brown eye with her hand.

GWEN

Like Brad Pitt.

She then covers the blue eye.

GWEN (cont'd) Like George Clooney.

Gwen smiles, looking at the whole Jack.

GWEN (cont'd)

I think I could get used to this.

Sam looks back at the Camera Crew and smiles.

GWEN (cont'd) You need to get some rest.

DISSOLVE TO

18. INT. HOSPITAL ROOM-NIGHT 18

C.U. Of Jack as he sleeps.

CUT TO:

19. EXT. WOOD CUTTING PILE - DREAM SEQUENCE #1-DUSK

19

KILLER's P.O.V. - he stalks GWEN (though we don't see her face-yet) through a FOG covered field. The frightened woman glances over her shoulder, then runs. (VIDEO EFFECTS THROUGHOUT, WITH JUMP CUTS OF THE TRACKING. EFFECT CAN BE USED TO SPEED US THROUGH THIS PROCESS, MAINTAINING KILLER'S

P.O.V.) The Killer chases, his heavy breathing being the dominant sound. He reaches out, grabs her, spins her around. CAMERA moves to the killer beofore we see her face. She struggles, then falls. The Killer's hands go around her neck. The CAMERA moves closer as her legs flail about.

CUT TO:

20. EXT. HOUSE - BACKYARD - EVENING 20

Jack, sitting by the pool, watches the sunset. He wears special SUNGLASSES that protect all around his eyes.

JACK

Come on. You're going to miss it!

Gwen exits the house, carrying two glasses and a BOTTLE OF CHAMPAGNE.

GWEN

(pointing to the sky) It's beautiful, isn't it?

JACK

I had forgotten how beautiful.

Gwen pops the cork.

GWEN

I know you don't usually drink, but this is worth celebrating.

Gwen pours the champagne and hands a glass to Jack.

JACK

I don't think I'll ever get tired of watching the sunset again.

GWEN

(toasting) To sunsets.

They toast. Jack takes off his sunglasses, revealing *those* eyes. He stares intensely toward the sun for the first time. He actually appears somewhat demented.

As Jack stares, he takes a gulp of champagne, nearly emptying the glass.

GWEN (cont'd)

Hey, take it easy, cowboy. It's only been a couple days.

(off Jack's defiant look) Sam said to keep the glasses on.

JACK

(relenting) Oh ... yeah.

Jack slips the sunglasses back on, then finishes his champagne with one more gulp. He sets the empty glass down. Gwen looks at it, incredulously.

JACK (cont'd)

I don't want to wait - let's get married now - let's just do it.

GWEN

(beat)

Of course I want to - but you know I've got to make arrangements.

JACK

You've got vacation time due. Besides -

(with a smile)

- it'll be good for your psych classes to learn how to deal with separation anxiety.

Gwen meets Jack's look, and his smile. She nods.

CUT TO:

21. EXT. CAMPUS - DAY 21

Establish.

22. INT. UNIVERSITY LECTURE HALL - DAY 22

Gwen talks to her class.

GWEN

Incidents of high stress will drive some to extreme behavior. No example reflects this better than that of a psychopath, who will loose control of all rational thinking and therefore all control under *extreme* duress.

Gwen looks at the clock. It's the top of the hour.

GWEN (cont'd)

Read chapter 14 on Sigmund Freud and be prepared for a quiz.

GROANS

Jack, wearing his sunglasses, enters and waits by the door as the class leaves. Gwen finally notices him.

GWEN (cont'd) This is a nice surprise.

Jack walks into the classroom as the students file out.

JACK

I thought we could talk.

GWEN

Yeah? About what.

JACK

I thought we could talk about marriage.

GWEN

(smiling)

How about talking about our honeymoon?

JACK

Alright. So what'd ya got?

Gwen pulls out a Tahiti and Caribbean brochure.

GWEN

Depends on how far away you want to go. I was thinking ...

Jack notices the corner of a brochure buried in the pile. (DIRECTOR'S NOTE: it is important that we see Jack's eyes move to the brochure; important that we see Jack's P.O.V. of brochure; followed by Jack reacting to what he has seen). He pulls out the BROCHURE OF THE LIGHTHOUSE RESORT.

JACK

(interrupting) What's this?

Gwen takes the brochure.

GWEN

I'm not sure how this even got in here.

(turns it over)

Oh, that's right. I wrote the name of a restaurant on it - the one the travel agent told us to try if we go to Hawaii.

Gwen starts to toss the brochure away, but Jack stops her.

JACK

I like this. It looks good.

Gwen looks at the brochure.

GWEN

The Lighthouse Resort? It's in the Delta region, not far from here.

JACK

See if we can get a reservation.

GWEN

Really? We always talked about a tropical paradise.

Jack gives Gwen a strange smile.

JACK

As long as we're together.

Gwen looks at the brochure again. CAMERA PANS to the Lighthouse Resort brochure. PUSH IN THEN HOLD (LOCK DOWN)

DISSOLVE TO:

23. EXT. VIEW OF LIGHTHOUSE RESORT - FROM FERRY - DAY 23

WE BEGIN WITH A MATCH TO THE BROCHURE, the resort as we saw it before.

PULL BACK to reveal Jack and Gwen by the railing of the upper deck, looking toward the resort. Jack wears his sunglasses.

GWEN

There it is.

JACK

Pretty as a picture. And the best thing is, we'll practically have the island to ourselves.

GWEN

I suppose that's the advantage to taking a honeymoon off season.

Jack turns to survey the near empty deck of the ferry. The only people on board are the CREW and a half dozen other PASSENGERS. Leaning against the railing next to Gwen is BOBBY, a man in his 20s.

GWEN (cont'd)

Not many people on board today. Are you staying at the resort?

BOBBY

No. I work there. This is how it is this time of year. During the summer this boat makes three trips a day - filled to capacity. Come the end of the year she only makes one trip a day.

GWEN

(to Jack)

That means we're going to have a lot of alone time.

(smiles) I'm excited.

JACK

(aside, to Gwen)

I had a feeling he wasn't a guest.

GWEN

Why?

JACK

Notice the boots. Work boots - and he's alone.

GWEN

Aren't you the observant one.

JACK

My new hobby. People watching. (motioning with his head)

Tell me what you see.

P.O.V. of GRETCHEN, a middle-aged woman, reading a BOOK.

GWEN

A woman reading a book.

JACK

(correcting her)

A woman who lives on the island, works at the resort. She makes this trip often, so often she's bored with it. That's why she's reading - and she's interested in dark things, the macabre.

(off Gwen's curious look) Notice the book.

Gwen sees the title: *Murder, Mayhem and Serial Killers*.

JACK (cont'd)

Not your normal "chick lit" fare.

Jack motions toward a couple standing by the railing on the other side of the deck.

JACK (cont'd) Now, there's a happy couple.

Jack's P.O.V. of the BIGLER's, NED and MAMIE. He's a bit of a nerd who holds, and is very protective of, a METAL DETECTOR. She's a bit of a nag, as she berates him about bringing his "stupid toy."

RETURN to Jack and Gwen.

JACK (cont'd)

Well ... maybe not so happy. Let's try not to sit near them at dinner.

The FERRY WHISTLE SOUNDS.

24. EXT. DOCK - DAY 24

Jack, Gwen, Bigler, his wife Mamie, Bobby and a few others disembark. Gretchen also leaves, but walks past everyone on her way to the resort. Waiting to greet the group of tourists and vacationers is CLARENCE BUTCHER, tour guide and resort rep.

Also, off to the side, we see SHERIFF ROY WHITMAN, middle age or older, he clearly has an agenda as he closely watches anyone new to the island.

CLARENCE

Welcome to the Delta's finest and most secluded couple's destination: The Lighthouse Resort.

Jack lowers his glasses. His eyes search the area. It all looks familiar to him.

CLARENCE (cont'd)

We have created an environment free from distractions, where the focus can be on each other ... the outside world can fade into the horizon.

You may as well turn those cell phones off, they don't work here.

Jack's gaze moves to a PAY PHONE BOOTH at the end of the dock.

GWEN

(quietly, to Jack) What's the matter?

JACK

Nothing. Just a feeling ... that I've been here ...

CLARENCE

Follow me folks, and I'll show ya'all to your bungalows.

Clarence points out a couple points of interest. Jack's eyes always seem to be one step ahead of him.

The Sheriff looks at Jack with suspicion. Jack sees this and puts his glasses back on, concealing his eyes.

Bigler, anxious to get away from his wife, pushes past Jack.

BIGLER

I heard there might be some buried treasure here.

CLARENCE

(smiles)

Well now, there is some folklore bout' all that but nothings been found, which is why I still work for a living.

Laughter from the small crowd. Bigler holds up his metal detector.

BIGLER

I'm hoping to find some.

CLARENCE

Good luck to you sir.

MAMIE

(annoyed)

Where can you get a drink around here?

CLARENCE

(chuckling)

You folks follow me and I'll show you.

Surprised by this, Gwen follows Jack.

CUT TO:

25. EXT. BUNGALOW-DAY 25

Establishing.

26. INT. BUNGALOW - DAY 26

Jack and Gwen arrive at their vacation home. Jack surveys the surroundings.

GWEN

I have to admit, maybe the Delta was a good idea!

JACK

No TV.

Gwen looks at a RECORD PLAYER and a SMALL STACK OF LP RECORD.

GWEN

Good.

Gwen turns on the record player and moves over to Jack, dancing around playfully. They share a long kiss.

CUT TO:

27. INT./EXT. LIGHTHOUSE RESTAURANT - PATIO - NIGHT 27

The restaurant's patio looks out onto the docks where

ILLUMINATED HOUSEBOATS float by on the marina. Gwen and Jack sit at a patio table. He drinks WHISKEY ON THE ROCKS. She sips WINE. Jack toasts Gwen.

JACK

To a new life - where everything will be different.

Gwen takes a sip. Concerned, she watches Jack down his drink.

GWEN

I'm surprised to see you drinking - especially whiskey. Do you think that's such a good idea?

JACK

You worry too much. I never noticed that about you before. You need to let your hair down.

GWEN

(a little suprised)

O.K.

Jack signals for another drink to the waiter (this is Bobby, who we met earlier).

Gwen smiles, feeling comforted by this old habit. She puts her hand on Jack's. He looks up.

GWEN (cont'd) I love you.

BOBBY (O.C.)

Here's your drink, sir.

Jack looks up at Bobby with *those eyes*. Bobby starts to react nervously, then catches himself.

BOBBY (cont'd)

Your food should be ready. I'll

... go check on it.

GWEN

(again) I love you...

CAMERA PUSHES in on Jack's face. His eyes are unflinching as he stares at beautiful large chested woman having dinner with her boyfriend

SMASH CUT TO:

28. INT. BATHROOM - SHOWER - FLASHBACK #1- NIGHT 28

Like a page out of “Psycho” - a man’s hand yanks open the

SHOWER CURTAIN, revealing a LOVELY WOMAN standing under the spray. This is FEMALE VICTIM #1. The TILE behind her has distinctive DECALS on it (which we will notice and remember when we see them again - and we will). The hands grab her and push her against the tile wall. One hand holds a KNIFE under her throat. The other hand runs it’s fingers through her wet SOAPY hair.

HORTON’S VOICE

Beautiful hair - the first thing I noticed when I saw you.

The hand yanks Female Victim #1’s hair. She SCREAMS as he cuts, the knife separating her “beautiful hair” from her skull. Her arms flail, hitting the man.

QUICK CUT TO:

29. EXT. RESTAURANT - PATIO - AS BEFORE 29

Bobby leans in with Jack's PLATE OF FOOD. Jack slaps it

away, reacting to the vision he's just had. The CRASH of the plate jars Jack back to reality. Every eye in the place is on him now.

In an attempt to reorientate himself, Jack looks around the room. He sees Bigler and his wife, staring. At the bar is CONGRESSMAN EDWARD DONALDS and his trophy wife, KARI (both whom we will meet later), and both staring. At another table is Sheriff Whitman, and Gretchen, the woman we saw earlier on the ferry, who is serving him a drink. Both stare.

RETURN - Bobby quickly drops to his knees to clean up the mess. Jack is embarrassed. Gwen is concerned.

GWEN

Are you okay?

JACK

I just need a drink.

CUT TO:

30. EXT. DOCK - LATER 30

Jack has his arm around Gwen as they walk. Jack sings,

happily drunk ("Show Me the Way To Go Home" maybe, which is a public domain drinking song). Gwen tries to have a good time.

GWEN

I do hope you remember this is our honeymoon...

(looking at the whiskey bottle)

...Mr. Jack.

JACK

Of course I do. Why do you think I was celebrating?

Gwen is silent. Jack is oblivious to her mood.

JACK (cont'd)

I have big plans for us, honey. I ordered champagne. It should be waiting for us when we get back.

CUT TO:

31. INT. BUNGALOW - BEDROOM - NIGHT - LATER 31

Gwen sits on the bed, wearing a beautiful negligee, drinking champagne - alone. O.C. Jack RETCHES. Gwen, annoyed, looks toward the bathroom.

32. INT. ADJOINING BATHROOM-CONTINUOUS 32

Jack's head is in the toilet, throwing up. Finished, he washes his face with cold water and looks in the mirror.

JACK

(to his reflection; quietly)

What's your problem, Jack? You didn't used to be such a jerk.

When Jack drops down to rinse his face again, the shower tile comes into focus in the mirror. It has the same distinct pattern as the tile in his earlier vision had. When Jack lifts his head, he sees this.

Jack stares at the shower in the mirror, then, leans out of frame and throws-up.

SMASH CUT to female victim #1 flashback from earlier.

C.U. Of blood washing down the shower drain.

CUT TO:

33. INT. BUNGALOW - BEDROOM - NIGHT - LATER 33

The DIGITAL CLOCK on the night stand reads 3:15 AM. Jack and Gwen are fast asleep. As we PUSH IN on Jack, he rolls over, putting his arm around Gwen to spoon her.

CUT TO:

34. INT. BUNGALOW - DINNING ROOM TABLE - NEXT DAY 34

Gwen is at the dinning room table, having a cup of coffee. Jack, wearing sunglasses, enters.

GWEN

Good morning, sunshine. Feeling better today?

Jack pours himself a cup of coffee with shaky hands. Gwen notices, but says nothing.

JACK

Yeah, I guess so. What exactly happened to me last night?

GWEN

You mean, when Jeckle became Hyde?

JACK

Was I that bad?

Gwen pats his hand reassuringly, trying to calm the trembling.

GWEN

You were celebrating.

JACK

Remind me not to celebrate anymore.

GWEN

You'll be okay. Let's just forget about last night, and have a fun day exploring the island.

JACK

(with a devilish smile) I'd rather explore you!

Jack pulls Gwen close, "exploring" her body, the passion quickly ignites. Jack carries Gwen to the DINING ROOM TABLE. They push the center piece off. Jack runs his fingers through her hair.

JACK (cont'd) Beautiful hair.

Jack sucks on Gwen's ear, then her neck and works his way down her body. This is a very different

Jack than the one we saw making love to Gwen before (with the blindfold). This time, he is driving the exchange with primal lust and even a hint of angry, reckless passion. Clothes do not get removed, they get torn from the body. Lips and flesh do not get kissed, they get sucked and bitten. As for Gwen, she is surprised and even intrigued. She does not resist. A series of EXTREME CLOSE-UPS and DISSOLVES speed us through this hedonistic exchange. Jack falls back onto a dining room chair, exhausted, satisfied. Gwen too is satisfied, although confused.

CUT TO:

35. EXT. NORTH SHORE - TRAIL - DAY 35

Jack, wearing sunglasses, chases Gwen through the trees.

Gwen laughs as Jack pretends to catch her, then lets her get away. Jack falls off in the background as Gwen continues to run. She pauses and returns to see:

Jack, by a DISTINCTIVE TREE, staring at the ground in a peculiar way. He squats down and traces the dirt (CAMERA PUSHES IN - MUSIC is OMINOUS).

GWEN

Lose something?

JACK

No ... I think I found something.

GWEN

What?

JACK

I don’t know.

Jack continues to touch the ground - almost caressing the soil. Gwen is puzzled as she watches Jack’s odd conduct.

Jack rises up, taking one last look at the spot on the ground. Then:

JACK (cont’d)

Let’s go.

Jack walks off toward the beach. Gwen looks back at the spot of ground.

36. EXT. NORTH SHORE - BEACH - DAY 36

Gwen relaxes on a BLANKET, soaking up the warm weather. Jack, wearing his sunglasses, sits next to her, looking somber. He stares blankly at the water.

JACK

(without turning)

I've been having bad dreams - ever since the operation.

(then)

There's this guy. He's always with a woman. It gets kind of rough - maybe she likes it - I'm not sure, but he's definitely in charge.

GWEN

Who is he?

JACK

I don't know - I can only see his hands... and the things he does ... the terrible things he does ...

Jack stares out at the water, his mind, somewhere else. Gwen watches him, concerned.

CUT TO:

37. INT. THE LIGHTHOUSE RESTAURANT - DAY 37

Jack and Gwen enter. Gwen spots a table and moves toward it - but Jack heads straight to the bar. Gwen almost calls him, then relents and follows.

At the bar is Sheriff Whitman, drinking and laughing with Congressman Ed Donalds and his wife, Kari.

Jack arrives at the bar. Seeing the Sheriff, Jack immediately puts his dark glasses on, just as Gwen catches up.

GWEN

Are we in cognito?

JACK

A little too much sun today, I guess. Feels better this way.

Gretchen approaches from the business side of the bar.

JACK (cont'd)

Whiskey on the rocks. White wine for the lady.

DONALDS

HELLO THERE! Welcome to the party! I'm Ed Donalds. This is my wife, Kari.

Jack nods, watching them without speaking, looking more at Kari's breasts than hearing what Donalds is saying.

GWEN

Congressman Donalds, isn't it?

DONALDS

Not tonight - not here. It's just Ed. One of the people.

KARI

(teasing)

One of the *drunk* people.

GWEN

Well, Ed, I'm Gwen, and this is my husband Jack. Nice to meet you.

Are you on your honeymoon as well?

DONALDS

That's right. Married two days ago. And they said it wouldn't last!

Donalds and Kari laugh. Jack continues to leer at Kari. Gretchen serves Jack and Gwen their drinks.

SHERIFF

You got yourself a keeper this time, Ed.

(holding up his drink) Here's to a happy union.

They all toast, then:

GWEN

I'm surprised we got the Grand Bungalow with you being newlyweds, too.

DONALDS

I brought my own bungalow - a Yacht. I never leave home without it.

GWEN

First time here, Ed?

DONALDS

No. I've been coming here for ... how long now, Gretchen - ten years?

GRETCHEN

Yep. Ever since the Horton murders.

GWEN

I’m sorry, someone was murdered here?

SHERIFF

(correcting her)

No one’s ever died on this island.

GRETCHEN

(sarcastic)

That’s right, they just go missing. It was three in one weekend as I recall.

SHERIFF

Ancient history.

GRETCHEN

Oh ... Maybe you’re right. That

was ten years ago.

The Sheriff relaxes, satisfied he’s soothed the beast.

GRETCHEN (cont’d) And they’re STILL missing.

The Sheriff shoots Gretchen a look that she brushes off.

DONALDS

(playing peace maker) Gretchen, be a doll and bring a round for everyone, on me, the Sheriff included. This is a night for celebration.

Gretchen walks away.

DONALDS (cont'd) (to the Newman's)

Nice girl, but reads too many mysteries.

Gwen politely smiles.

Jack notices a NECKLACE nestled between Kari's ample breasts.

JACK

Nice necklace you got there, Kari.

Gwen sees Jack's focus and tries to prevent embarrassment.

GWEN

Yes, it *is* beautiful.

KARI

Ed gave it to me.

INSERT - C.U. NECKLACE and plenty of impressive cleavage.

JACK

(staring at her breasts) Nice.

Gwen casts a sideways glance at Jack. As the drinks arrive:

DONALDS

I knew this was the girl for me the moment I saw her.

JACK

(still staring) I can see why.

Jack drains his drink. Gwen watches, disapprovingly.

Donalds and Kari playfully kiss each other. Gwen turns away, speaking privately to Jack.

GWEN

Will you behave yourself and slow down on the drinking?! We don't want a repeat of last night.

JACK

It's a celebration, right?

GWEN

I thought we *weren't* going to celebrate anymore.

JACK

There's plenty of time to not celebrate when we get home - loosen up, will you?

Jack slaps thc bar and takes off his sunglasses, revealing

those eyes.

JACK (cont'd)

Two more, straight up this time.

Jack starts tidying up anything he can find on the bar, almost manically. Gwen notices this, then sees the Sheriff has noticed, too.

GWEN

(whispering) Jack, just let it go?

Jack ignores Gwen. The Sheriff stares.

CUT TO:

38. EXT. BUNGALOW - POOL - THE NEXT MORNING38

Gwen reads the NEWSPAPER as she sips COFFEE.

The patio door opens. An aloof Jack, wearing sunglasses and his ROBE, approaches. He picks up a section of the newspaper and sits next to Gwen.

JACK

How did you sleep last night?

Silence.

JACK (cont'd) What's wrong?

Gwen looks at him for a moment and chooses her words carefully.

GWEN

It's our honeymoon. You get drunk every night, make an ass out of yourself, then come back here and pass out. What's wrong with *me*?

What's wrong with *you*?

Jack starts to straighten items on the table.

GWEN (cont'd) (frustrated)

Will you stop that and listen to me?!

Jack stops and looks at Gwen.

GWEN (cont'd) (trying to calm down, but

not well)

We are on our honeymoon and I want us to have some fun together!

JACK

If you want to have fun, why don't we go out on a boat.

GWEN

(pause)

Well, alright. But I'm not ready yet.

JACK

Then I'll go check it out.

Jack tosses the paper. He stares at Gwen for a moment before exiting, leaving Gwen speechless.

CUT TO:

39. EXT. DOCK - DAY 39

Kari Donalds, in revealing bikini, sunbathes on the upper

deck of her boat. Jack, wearing sunglasses, slows to take in the scenery.

Noticing Jack, Kari lowers her sunglasses to regard him. She smiles slyly and waves her fingers in a seductive hello.

Congressman Donalds appears, staring at him. Jack's expression hardens at the interruption, then continues walking.

40. EXT. OLD DOCK - DAY 40

Jack, still in sunglasses, strolls on the OLD DOCK - this area used by the locals, not tourists.

ANGLE - FURTHER DOWN DOCK

GRADY, a man in his sixties, watches Jack like a hawk.

JACK

(taking off sunglasses) Hey, Pops, I understand you got boats for rent.

Grady looks Jack over, not appreciating be called "Pops."

GRADY

Sure, they're for rent. Need them to come back, though. We share this here waterway with that fancy resort, and one of their guests drowning in my boat is trouble I don't need.

JACK

How much for this one?

Jack points to a SPEED BOAT.

GRADY

Seventy five dollars a day.

Jack tosses SEVERAL BILLS onto the counter. Grady stares for a moment until finally grabbing a KEY from the cabinet.

GRADY (cont'd)

Just try not to drown out there, I don't need no Sheriff grillin' my ass.

Grady watches him cast off, fire up the outboard motor, and speed away. Jack shoots Grady a confident look as he leaves.

GRADY (cont'd)

Smart ass.

41. INT./EXT. BOAT - ON THE WATER - MOMENTS LATER41

Jack revs the engine, building up speed as he captains through the Marina.

42. EXT. BUNGALOW PATIO - MOMENTS LATER 42

Jack rounds the bend and passes his bungalow. Gwen, still by the pool sees him. As he passes, she throws down her sunglasses and storms back to the house.

CUT TO:

43. EXT. BOAT - DAY 43

Jacks speeds through the Delta. After a few moments he

notices a place to dock on shore and pilots the boat in that direction.

CUT TO:

44. EXT. NORTH SHORE - DAY 44

The speed boat is tied off at the end of the shore. Jack

stands on the trail, looking at the same spot of loose dirt under a familiar tree from earlier.

45. EXT. NORTH SHORE - TRAIL AREA - DAY 45

At the foot of the distinctive tree, Jack surveys the area. He squats down and touches the dirt. Then rises up, eyes still on the ground, obsessed with the grave like dirt.

E.C.U. Jack, as he removes his glasses - those intense eyes stare.

As Jack begins to leave he comes face to face with Ned Bigler, the metal detector guy. Jack lets out a GASP, scaring Bigler.

BIGLER

Holy shit, you scared me half to death!

JACK

What are you doing?

Bigler looks around, baffled.

BIGLER

What?

JACK

What are you doing here right now?

Jack glares at Bigler. Those eyes are back, brighter than usual - penetrating, threatening. Bigler swallows.

BIGLER

I was just checking along the trail for metal. You know, rings, watches, coins, the sort of things people lose. You'd be surprised

...

Bigler activates the METAL DETECTOR and immediately gets a signal. He looks toward the ground in front of the old tree.

BIGLER (cont'd)

There might be something over there

...

Bigler sees the look on Jack's face and decides to back off.

JACK

I think you'd be better sticking closer to the resort.

Jack's eyes burn a hole through Bigler, who nervously moves on. Jack waits until he is alone, then looks back to where the grave was. The dirt remains undisturbed.

CUT TO:

46. EXT. MARINA - AFTERNOON 46

Gwen walks toward the island's only PHONE BOOTH.

47. ANGLE - PAY PHONE 47

Gwen feeds the pay phone with coins, then dials.

OPERATOR'S VOICE

(over phone, FILTERED) Optometry.

GWEN

(into phone)

Dr. Sam Rieland, please. Tell him it's Gwen Newman - it's important.

OPERATOR'S VOICE (FILTERED)

Please hold.

Several "on hold" beeps are heard as Gwen looks out and sees MIKA, a local man, gutting a large fish. Squeamish, Gwen turns away.

SAM'S VOICE (FILTERED)

Gwen, how's my star patient doing?

GWEN

Well, that's just it ...

INTERCUT WITH:

48. INT. SAM'S OFFICE - DAY 48

Sam talks on phone. He's got a MAGAZINE open to a page with a PICTURE OF HIMSELF and a headline "New Visionary Brings Gift Of Sight." He holds the magazine as:

SAM

(interrupts)

You'd better tell Jack to enjoy his privacy while he still has it - he's been making quite a stir with the press.

GWEN

Sam, there may be a problem ... Jack's been having ... complications.

Sam puts the magazine down.

SAM

What type of complications?

GWEN

Mood shifts, nightmares ... He's just not acting like himself ...

SAM

(interrupts)

His vision. Is he seeing alright?

GWEN

Yes ... I don't know ... he hasn't said anything about that. It's his behavior - it's not Jack - not the Jack I know.

Sam considers Gwen's words, as well as his response to them.

SAM

You know, Gwen ... it's not uncommon for an organ transplant recipient to act out of the ordinary for a time after an operation. And this represents a big change for Jack. He's trying to adjust to seeing for the first time in years.

GWEN

You're not talking to a layman, Sam. I understand psychology. You know that.

SAM

I also know that Jack isn't the only one who's been under a lot of pressure lately - with this operation - and all the changes.

(then)

Gwen, just give him a little time to get reacquainted with everything. He's probably putting a lot of pressure on himself to return to how he was years ago, but that's not something he'll be able to do overnight.

Gwen listens patiently - and, as she sees Jack's SPEEDBOAT in the distance:

GWEN

(ignoring what he's said)

Is there anything you can tell me about the donor? Did he drink?

SAM

Drink?

(guarded)

How would I know a thing like that?

GWEN

Jack's been drinking - a lot.

SAM

I've never known Jack to drink much. Nothing beyond an occasional glass of wine.

GWEN

That's the thing - it isn't making any sense to me, either.

(MORE)

GWEN (cont'd)

Can you find something/*anything* out about the donor?

SAM

Gwen, we don't have access to personal information regarding the donor. Even if I could, it would be unethical for ...

GWEN

(interrupting)

Please - just see what you can find out. I'll call you tomorrow.

SAM

Gwen ...

GWEN

Do it for Jack. Do it for me. I'm desperate, Sam.

Gwen hangs up.

49. INT. SAM'S OFFICE - CONTINUOUS 49

SAM

Gwen ...

Reacting the to DIAL TONE, Sam hangs up. Troubled over this development, he flips the magazine closed with a degree of temperament.

50. EXT. DOCK - PHONE BOOTH - DAY 50

Gwen exits the booth.

Mika holds up a LARGE FISH for Gwen.

MIKA

Fresh fish here.

Gwen reacts with disgust. Mika senses this. He puts the fish on his makeshift counter, and picks up a CLEAVER.

CHOP - The fish head falls off. Appalled, Gwen leaves.

CUT TO:

51. EXT. DOCK - EVENING 51

Jack, wearing his sunglasses, stares at the Donalds' boat.

JACK'S P.O.V. - THROUGH WINDOW INTO CABIN OF BOAT

Donalds is seated with his back to CAMERA. Kari stands in front of him. She dances seductively for the Congressman.

Jack watches.

Kari, seeing past her husband and out the window at Jack, becomes more sexual in her dancing. Donalds, oblivious to Jack, claps, encouraging his wife on.

Jack's face is expressionless. We PAN DOWN to see that he is slowly and methodically pulverizing the fish, seemingly, without realizing it.

CUT TO:

52. INT. BUNGALOW - FRONT ROOM & KITCHENETTE - DAY 52

Jack enters. He tosses his sunglasses down, recklessly,

ignoring Gwen. Jack takes a BOTTLE OF BOOZE out of a cabinet and pours himself a drink. Gwen takes notice of his strange activities.

GWEN

What are you doing? (off his silence)

Are you not speaking to me now?

Jack ignores her, enjoying his drink.

GWEN (cont'd)

I think we need to have a talk.

Gwen moves to the kitchen -

GWEN (cont'd)

What's going on with you, Jack?

JACK

I don't know what you mean.

Jack pours himself another drink.

GWEN

And this drinking - Jack.

Furious, Gwen grabs the bottle and tosses it in the sink.

HANDHELD of Jack walking away from Gwen as she follows him through the house.

GWEN (cont'd)

I thought we could talk about today.

JACK

And what about today do you want to talk about?

GWEN

(hesitant)

You've been acting ... very strange, Jack ... different.

JACK

So you keep saying. Tell me, doctor, if I'm not acting like myself, then who am I acting like?

GWEN

Like someone I've never met. Like someone I wouldn't want to meet.

Jack smiles, but Gwen's silent stare turns the condescending grin into open hostility.

JACK

A guy tries to have a little fun on his honeymoon and he turns into Mr. Fucking Hyde. Is that it? IS THAT WHAT YOU'RE TRYING TO SAY, GWEN?

Gwen's eyes fill with tears as she searches for a response.

GWEN

It's just ... ever since you got your eyes ... it's like ...

The tears come.

GWEN (cont'd)

Do I disappoint you that much, Jack? Do you not like what you see?

Jack walks to the counter and pours himself another drink.

JACK

It's all about you, isn't it? I guess I should expect that from a psych teacher. Maybe I want to have a little bit of freedom - some long overdue fun.

Gwen takes the bottle away from Jack and tosses it in the trash.

GWEN

Then why don't you go have your fun somewhere else!

Jack grabs Gwen and pushes her back against the wall. He holds her, his face a mere inch from hers. His breathing, harsh. She doesn't dare breath at all. Jack blinks, rubs his forehead, then eases up a bit.

JACK

(transforming back; a subtle change)

That sounds like a good idea. Jack releases Gwen. His look softens.

JACK (cont'd)

Stay away from me, Gwen. For your own good.

Jack exits the room. Gwen sinks to her knees and sobs.

CUT TO:

53. INT. RESTAURANT BAR - NIGHT 53

Jack, who is visibly agitated, enters. Kari and Ed Donalds are at the end of the bar. Donalds obviously has had too much to drink. Gretchen tends bar.

DONALDS

(inebriated)

I have the most beautiful wife, don't I Gretchen?

GRETCHEN

(rolling her eyes) Beautiful.

DONALDS

I want to dance with my beautiful wife.

Donalds tries to stand, but stumbles. Kari catches him.

KARI

Come on, baby, let's get you back to the boat. We'll do our dancing there.

Jack sits at the bar as Kari helps her husband to the door. She casts Jack a glance of recognition, which he returns.

Gretchen approaches Jack.

GRETCHEN

(RE: Donalds and Kari)

He was better off with the last wife. Plain as a post, but at least she didn't hiss when she smiled.

(then, to business) What'll it be?

JACK

Just give me a drink - WHISKEY.

Gretchen goes for the drink. Jack stares after Kari.

CUT TO:

54. EXT. DOCK - PHONE BOOTH - NIGHT 54

A sobbing Gwen talks on the phone.

GWEN

I don't know what's happening, Sam - the look in his eyes - for a moment, it felt like he wanted to kill me.

INTERCUT WITH:

55. INT. SAM'S OFFICE - NIGHT 55

Sam has a FILE laid out on his desk which includes a PICTURE OF TERRENCE LEE HORTON.

SAM

Just calm down. I understand how upset you are. When you come back I'll talk to Jack. I'll prescribe something to help with the mood shifts.

GWEN

I don't think he's going to come back - at least not with me ... I mean ... he's not the same - I'm afraid he's going to hurt someone.

(sobbing; beat)

(MORE)

GWEN (cont'd)

Did you find out anything about the donor?

Sam closes Horton's file.

SAM

No.

(beat)

We don't need to do a witch hunt here. Maybe you can do something to help, Gwen. You have a degree in psychology, start talking to him like a psychologist - take control.

GWEN

I'll try, but he doesn't listen now.

SAM

Maybe I should come out, we can work together. If I left now I could be there in the morning.

GWEN

Sam, really - you'd do that?

SAM

Try to stay calm. We'll find a way to make this right.

GWEN

Thank you, Sam.

SAM

I'll see you in the morning.

Sam hangs up. The look on his face is not the look of a friend.

CUT TO:

56. EXT. DOCKS - LATER 56

Jack stands outside the Donalds' boat - waiting.

On the top deck is Kari, drinking wine, enjoying the night sky. She turns, noticing Jack.

KARI

Ahoy there. What are you doing out this late? That wife of yours must be pretty careless.

JACK

She's not the late night party type. Looks like your husband isn't, either.

KARI

Fast asleep down below, dead to the world. I've warned him about vodka. Makes him comatose.

JACK

Damn shame. Looks like you and I have the same problem.

KARI

(smiling)

Well, you know what they say about mutual problems - misery loves company. Care to join me for a nightcap before I go below?

JACK

Sure. One last drink won't hurt anybody. Right?

Jack climbs aboard. Kari pours him a glass of wine.

KARI

So ... did you know your wife was a stick in the mud before you married her?

JACK

Actually, I was blind to it. But, the way I see it, now, is we only have one life ... and we should really experience everything.

Jack takes the wine from Kari.

JACK (cont'd)

You agree?

Kari notices his naughty look. This is fun for her, but only to a point.

KARI

I'd have to say that marriage has allowed me to experience more.

Ed's been very good to me. Very generous.

JACK

Sounds like an ideal arrangement - especially when he sleeps.

Kari smiles and casts Jack a sly look. She stands to refill her glass, Jack moves behind her. His breath increasing as he places his hands on her hips. She smiles, but ...

KARI

There's a time and a place for everything.

JACK

Daddy Congressman's not going to wake up - not unless you start screaming.

KARI

I'm not the screaming type.

JACK

All the better.

Jack pulls Kari to him - kisses her. She pulls away.

KARI

This is really not a good idea.

As Kari tries to move past Jack, he presses against her, kissing harder. She permits it for a moment, then, pulls back.

KARI (cont'd)

Listen, lover boy ...

Jack kisses her again, moving his hand up the front of Kari's blouse. She resists.

KARI (cont'd)

You're going to make trouble for me.

JACK

Something tells me you're the kind of girl who likes a little trouble.

KARI

Not when it threatens my livelihood.

Kari peels Jack's hand off her breasts.

KARI (cont'd)

Those cost me a lot of money - And you don't look like the type who can afford them.

Unfazed, Jack presses forward. Kari backs away, toward the stern of the boat. She hits the rail and teeters, a mixture of fear and intoxication. Jack grabs for her, instead he gets her necklace. Kari loses her balance. She SCREAMS as she falls into the water. The necklace still in Jack's hand.

Jack looks over the railing. Kari flails, the cold water takes her breath away, choking back her yell for help.

KARI (cont'd) (strained)

Help me!

JACK

I thought you said you weren't the screaming type?

KARI

I can't swim!

JACK

(Re: her breasts)

With those you ought to float.

Kari sinks.

JACK (cont'd) Or, maybe not.

(watching where Kari was) I'd like to have something to remember you by -

Jack looks to the necklace in his hand.

JACK (cont'd)

- Guess this will have to do.

CUT TO:

57. INT. BUNGALOW - LIVING ROOM - LATE NIGHT 57

Gwen sits in the shadows, waiting. Her expression tells us she is calmer, determined, ready.

Jack enters and almost walks by Gwen before he notices her presence.

JACK

Well, well. Miss me?

GWEN

It's 3 AM, Jack.

JACK

Now you're keeping track of my hours? How charming.

GWEN

I've been keeping track of more than that. You've become a bit of a paradox.

JACK

Uh oh, sounds like it's shrink time.

GWEN

(disregarding his sarcasm) Your losing control Jack.

JACK

I *have* control.

Jack steps up to the bar and pours a drink.

GWEN

The increased drinking. You're just trying to take control-like you're losing it somehow.

Jack stares at the drink for a moment before holding it out for Gwen.

JACK

Drink, doc?

GWEN

I'm serious about this, Jack.

JACK

I can see that. You've got a real pickle up your ass, Gwen. Maybe it's time somebody pulled it out.

Jack grabs Gwen and yanks her out of the chair.

GWEN

Knock it off!

JACK

Don't be so stiff.

GWEN

You're hurting me!

JACK

Believe me, Gwen-I'm not. Not yet, anyway.

Jack slaps Gwen across her face. Her nose bleeds. Intrigued by the blood, Jack wipes it off her face and smears it between his fingers. As Gwen cowers:

JACK (cont'd)

There are different degrees of hurt, Gwen. That was one level - this is another.

Jack throws Gwen on the couch. He starts ripping her cloths off.

GWEN

What are you doing?!

JACK

I think it should be very clear what I'm doing.

Jack continues to tear cloths off .

GWEN

What's wrong with you? Stop it!

JACK

Stop? I'm just getting started.

But Jack does stop - suddenly. He feels an intense pain in his temples. He tries to continue with the rape - but, in a moment of Jeckyl/Hyde struggle, Jack GASPS in pain. He rises off Gwen and staggers out of the house. Relieved, but confused, Gwen puts her skirt back in place.

58. EXT. BUNGALOW - POOL AREA - NIGHT 58

Jack - and he's the good Jack for this brief moment -

staggers from the house. With a nod to Hamlet, Jack rubs his blood stained hands together, frantically. He drops to his knees and submerges his hands in the water, trying to wash his sins away. He becomes light-headed and falls into the pool.

ANGLE - TO INCLUDE UPPER DECK

Reacting to the splash, Gwen rushes out and spots Jack floating on top of the water.

GWEN

Oh my God! Jack? Jack!

Gwen races down the stairs and jumps into the pool. She pulls Jack's head out of the water. With great effort, she finally gets him out of the pool and performs CPR. Soon, Jack COUGHS and GASPS for breath. He struggles to clear his lungs ... and his mind.

GWEN (cont'd)

That does it. I'm getting you out of this place. We're going home.

JACK

(sobbing) She's dead.

GWEN

What? Who's dead?

JACK

She's dead. It was an accident, but I let her drown. I wanted to help, but ...

Jack sobs and takes Kari's necklace out of his pocket.

JACK (cont'd)

I reached for her, she was falling - all I got was this.

GWEN

(recognizing it) That's Kari's.

Gwen looks at her sobbing husband. For the first time in days she feels pity for him, and takes him in her arms.

CUT TO:

59. INT. BUNGALOW - SHOWER - NIGHT 59

We SLOWLY DOLLY into the bathroom where the sound of running water and steam fill the air. Gwen sits on the shower floor, naked, knees pulled close to her chest and arms wrapped around her legs. She cries hysterically staring straight ahead past CAMERA.

ANGLE GWEN'S P.O.V. through the open door to the BEDROOM. Jack lies in bed, sleeping. He tosses and turns in the throws of another nightmare.

ANGLE GWEN - She is almost numb to what she sees, but continues to watch.

ANGLE BEDROOM - close on Jack. As he battles with his dream the CAMERA pushes in -

DISSOLVE TO:

60. EXT. OPEN FIELD-DREAM SEQUENCE #2-DUSK 60

We return to the nightmare in the field.

Terrence Lee Horton, only a few feet away from Jack, cracks the neck of his female victim. Terrence turns to Jack. He has no eyes, just dark empty sockets where eyes should be. Disturbed by this, Jack turns to the swollen and bloody victim.

C.U. REVEAL the lifeless face staring back at Jack is Gwen!

Jack closes his eyes in horror, only to find when he opens them again, it is his own hands which twist the neck of his dead wife.

CUT TO:

61. EXT. PRIVATE DOCK (OLD DOCK) - DAY 61

Earl and Dell are on the deck of their boat, nearby.

Sam, dressed for travel, carries a SMALL BAG as he steps off the SMALL SHUTTLE BOAT. Sam's CELL PHONE rings. He pulls it out of his pocket and answers.

SAM

Hello? ... Gwen? ... I Can hardly hear you. Hello?

Earl and Dell notice.

EARL

You don't get no signal out here. There's a pay phone on the newer dock - by the resort - half mile that way.

SAM

Actually, I just need directions. I'm looking for two friends of mine. One of them might be wearing dark glasses. They arrived a couple of days ago.

EARL

(taking a moment) Oh, them two.

DELL

She's a pretty one. Anyone would notice her.

EARL

They're stayin' at the "big house" - up there on that hill ...

(pointing)

... the two story one, past all them little bungalows.

SAM

Thank you.

Sam walks off.

CUT TO:

62. INT. BUNGALOW - FRONT DOOR - AFTERNOON 62

The front door is ajar. Sam knocks, then pokes his head in.

SAM

Hello? Gwen? Jack?

OPERA MUSIC can be heard O.C. - Sam follows the sound to:

63. INT. GAME ROOM - MOMENTS LATER63

Jack sits at the wet bar facing camera. He slices LIMES with a LARGE KNIFE. His back is to the door. The source of the music, the old record player, sits on the bar. In the background, behind Jack, Sam steps into the doorway.

SAM

Oh, there you are.

Jack pauses from cutting the lime. His head raises slightly. A small smile cuts through his face. Without turning to face Sam:

JACK

Hello, Sam. What a surprise.

SAM

Gwen didn't tell you I was coming?

JACK

It must have slipped her mind - but how nice that you're here. Join me for a drink - you're a Martini man as I recall.

Jack takes out a Martini glass.

SAM

It's a little early for that.

JACK

Suit yourself.

Jack picks up his own drink and turns to face Sam.

Sam can't help but react to Jack's transformation - it is deranged, maniacal. Feeling uneasy, Sam shifts his attention to the music playing.

SAM

(picking up a record) Opera? You?

JACK

Funny. Gwen said it that way, too - exactly that way. But you see, Sam

- I've been expanding my interests - discovering new things.

Jack stares at Sam, making him uncomfortable.

JACK (cont'd)

I didn't know you made house calls.

SAM

Sure I do, Jack, for my very close friends.

Jack gets up from his seat and moves toward Sam.

JACK

Are we close friends, doc? Really close friends?

Nervous, Sam looks around at his options.

SAM

Of course we are.

Jack moves in closer.

JACK

Here's what I think you are - an opportunist. I think you just want to be on the news. Well, Sam, it's your lucky day. I'm going to make it happen for you.

Jack holds up the lime knife.

Sam runs for the door. Jack steps in between, blocking Sam's way. Sam spies another doorway at the other end of the room and bolts. It leads upstairs.

Jack follows. At the bottom of the stairs he smiles, calls out:

JACK (cont'd)

Think you're smart, don't you, Sam? Let's try this again - from the top.

Jack slowly ascends the stairs.

64. INT. BEDROOM - AFTERNOON 64

Sam runs in and grabs a LAMP.

(POST NOTE: OPERA MUSIC builds, adding surrealism and tension to the scene)

65. INT. HALLWAY - DAY 65

Jack reaches the top of the stairs. A smile spreads across his face. He moves to the bedroom.

66. INT. BEDROOM - CONTINUOUS 66

Sam, breathing hard, listens for Jack. His hand tightens around the lamp, sweat beads on his forehead.

JACK (O.C.)

Doc, you shouldn't be afraid of me.

Jack steps into the doorway.

JACK (cont'd) You made me.

Sam swings the lamp. Jack deflects the blow, knocking the lamp out of Sam's hands while backing him against the wall.

JACK (cont'd)

So what do you have to say for yourself, “friend?”

Sam starts to speak, but Jack covers his mouth with his hand.

JACK (cont’d)

I wouldn’t believe anything you said, anyway. Only ...

Jack moves closer to Sam.

JACK (cont’d) (whispering)

... seeing ...

Even closer.

JACK (cont’d) (whispering)

... is ...

Nose to nose with Sam. Jack’s eyes wide open.

JACK (cont’d) (whispering)

... BELIEVING.

CUT TO:

67. EXT. OLD DOCKS - DAY 67

A CROWD has gathered. Two or three locals haul Kari’s body out of the water as the Sheriff watches.

A distraught and disoriented Ed Donalds sits in shock as Mamie tries to comfort him. Dell and Earl are nearby, both clearly shaken.

Gwen pushes through the crowd, arriving next to Gretchen, who is fascinated with the event. Gretchen looks over to Gwen.

GRETCHEN

Sure has drawn a crowd. Just about everyone on the island is here.

Pretty exciting, huh?

GWEN

What?

As we see the Sheriff walks to Earl and Dell:

GRETCHEN

(to Gwen) Shhh!

ANGLE - SHERIFF AT EDGE OF DOCK

SHERIFF

Tell me about it, boys.

DELL

We was fishin' off the pier when Earl hooked what he thought was a sea lion, but it was that woman ...

Dell points to Kari's body.

EARL

I never expected nothin' like this.

The Sheriff goes to inspect the body. Bobby (from the restaurant) takes the hook out of her body.

SHERIFF

(quietly; as he observes)

What do you think, Bobby? I don't see any trauma to the body or head.

BOBBY

Just where Earl hooked her.

SHERIFF

Looks to me like an accidental drowning.

Dell steps up and looks over the Sheriff's shoulder.

DELL

Do you really think that's all it was, Sheriff - just a drowning?

SHERIFF

We don’t need to make more of this than it already is, Dell.

The Sheriff calls on his HAND RADIO.

SHERIFF (cont’d)

Maggie?

WOMAN’S VOICE

(over Hand Radio, filtered)

Go ahead, Sheriff.

SHERIFF

Tell Doc Craig I need him. Got a drowning - I’ll need a coroners report.

WOMAN’S VOICE

Roger that.

GRETCHEN (O.C.) (CALLS OUT)

Sheriff.

The Sheriff looks over. When he sees it’s Gretchen, he sighs.

ANGLE - TO INCLUDE GRETCHEN

GRETCHEN (cont’d)

I just want to let you know ... they were both at the bar last night.

(to Donalds) No disrespect -

(back to Sheriff)

- but he was five sheets to the wind.

SHERIFF

(dismissing her) Thank you, Gretchen.

The Sheriff approaches Donalds.

SHERIFF (cont'd)

I sure am sorry about this, Ed. Is there anything you can tell me?

DONALDS

(sobbing)

She was okay last I saw her ... said she was just going back on deck for a nightcap before coming to bed. Then I woke up to this ...

ANGLE Gretchen and Gwen in crowd.

GRETCHEN

(aside to Gwen)

You know, your husband was there too, at the bar. I ain't sayin' he had anything to do with this - I'm just sayin' he was there.

Gwen reacts with concern and guilt. During this, Clarence pushes through the crowd.

CLARENCE

Get out of the way, I need to talk to the sheriff!

(CALLS OUT)

Sheriff! Sheriff, one of my guests just found a body on the trail off the North Shore.

The Crowd reacts. Clarence finally sees Kari's body.

CLARENCE (cont'd)

My God.

CUT TO:

68. EXT. NORTH SHORE TRAIL - AFTERNOON/EVENING 68

Bigler, with his metal detector, is here, and shaken up.

Clarence stands by as the Sheriff looks at the remains of a female corpse in the unearthed grave.

It is more skeleton then body. Gwen and a group of on-lookers, including Gretchen, make their way onto the scene, clamoring among themselves, and watching.

The Sheriff rises up and looks at Bigler.

BIGLER

It's terrible. I don't know how I'll ever get this image out of my mind. I don't know how ...

SHERIFF

Calm down. Tell me how you found her.

BIGLER

I started digging for metal- and that's when I saw it - a gold band with a diamond. I went to pick it up and there was a stick through it, like a root.

(MORE)

BIGLER (cont'd)

So I pulled on it - except it wasn't a root - it was a bone! Oh my god! I touched it! Don't you understand, I touched it!

Bigler is overwhelmed. Mamie moves in to comfort him. Clarence leans into the Sheriff.

CLARENCE

Hell, how we going to keep the lid on this one, Roy? Just about everyone on the island is here.

The Sheriff looks up.

SHERIFF

We'll think of something, Clarence. We always do.

ANGLE TO INCLUDE GRETCHEN

Gretchen, inching forward to where she is again standing next to Gwen, leans in and speaks to her.

GRETCHEN

Betcha' that ain't the only one. (off Gwen's questioning

look)

Three women turned up missing here a few years ago. They never found a single one of the bodies ... until now, anyway.

(excited)

It was that killer-Terrence Lee Horton - the one they executed a while back.

GWEN

How do you know that?

GRETCHEN

'Cause I saw him. No one forgets that face - with those eyes ... kinda like your husband's.

GWEN

(confused)

What are you talking about?

GWEN (cont'd) I'll show you.

CUT TO:

69. EXT. GRETCHEN'S HOUSE BOAT- AFTERNOON/EVENING 69

A dilapidated house boat. The shrubbery is overgrown, piles of junk stacked everywhere. Gretchen is clearly a "pack rat." As Gretchen leads Gwen to the door:

GRETCHEN

The Sheriff and the people who run the resort, they don't believe it. They don't get it. Murder is good for business - always has been.

Gretchen opens the door.

70. INT. GRETCHEN'S HOUSE BOAT - AFTERNOON - CONTINUOUS 70

An eye sore. NEWSPAPERS are stacked to the ceiling. News

CLIPPINGS "decorate" the walls. All articles concern serial killings.

GRETCHEN

Of course, I didn't know who he was when he was here. That came later, after he was arrested and they started running his picture in the papers.

Gwen leans in and looks at the wall filled with clippings. It's a mess - everything is taped and tacked in no discernible order. Most contain mug shots of Horton intently staring into camera. There are 3 FRAMED PICTURES on the wall. (NOTE: 2 these pictures are in black and white and do not reveal the color of his eyes. The last one- in color- does).

As Gwen looks at the pictures:

GRETCHEN (cont'd)

He killed 13 women that they know of. But you know there's got to be more. He always took a piece of them that represented their personality.

(off Gwen's disgusted look)

I've made it my hobby to study men like him.

(MORE)

GRETCHEN (cont'd)

A pretty girl can't be too careful. (motions)

This ought to interest you.

Gretchen points Gwen to a FRAMED PHOTO which hangs on the wall. It shows a group of people, in the bar of the island restaurant, smiling and toasting the camera.

GRETCHEN'S VOICE (O.S.)

This was taken the week those women vanished. Here's one ... and another ... and the third.

Gretchen points to each of the three women, one of which we've seen before - Female Victims 1-and two unknown women.

GRETCHEN

There was a big party in the main ballroom. It was the Fourth of July.

Gwen noticcs a youngcr Gretchen in the photo.

GRETCHEN (cont'd)

I was workin' that night - but, then, I didn't end up dead neither.

Gwen leans in and sees Horton among the revelers. The color image of his eyes sends a shiver up her spine. Gwen takes it off the wall.

GRETCHEN (cont'd)

Of course, I brought this to the Sheriff's attention. But his job is to just make sure people keep coming to the island.

Gwen's face reads her moment of realization as she drops the color photo and rushes out. Disappointed, Gretchen calls after her:

GRETCHEN (cont'd) They'll have to listen to me, now. You can bet there'll be plenty more excitement 'round here! You'll see!

CUT TO:

71. EXT. BUNGALOW - NIGHT 71

Gwen hurries back, rushing through the front door.

72. INT. BUNGALOW - CONTINUOUS 72

OPERA MUSIC PLAYS.

Gwen cautiously proceeds into the house and sees Sam's overnight bag on the floor. Gwen reacts to the music.

GWEN

Sam?

Gwen moves deeper into the house.

73. INT. BUNGALOW - GAME ROOM - CONTINUOUS 73

The OPERA MUSIC is louder. This is the source. Gwen steps in and reacts to a vision of the "Old Jack," friendly, happy, non-threatening.

Sitting across from Jack, with his back toward us and Gwen, is Sam. In between them on the wet bar are two drinks. One is a MARTINI.

Jack looks up, seeing Gwen, he smiles.

JACK

Gwen, look who's here. It's our good friend.

Relieved, Gwen hurries forward.

GWEN

Sam, I'm so happy to see ...

Gwen freezes in her tracks. Sam is dead, propped up in the chair with bloody holes where his eyes should be.

JACK

We were just having a drink. Join us.

Jack motions to the martini glass where SAM'S EYEBALLS float, staring out at Gwen. Gwen GASPS. Jack smiles as Gwen bolts out the door.

CUT TO:

74. EXT. BUNGALOW DOCK - NIGHT 74

Gwen frantically runs down the ramp toward the docks. There is no one in sight. A BOAT piloted by Earl and Dell passes. Gwen races to the edge of the dock and calls out.

GWEN

Help! Please, help me!

Earl cups his ear.

EARL (CALLING OUT)

What?

GWEN (YELLING)

I need your help! A man's been killed!

EARL

I know, they found another body!

DELL

That's three in one day!

GWEN

I need help!

Still not hearing, Earl points, calls out one last time.

Gwen looks around anxiously. She spots the pay phone and hurries to it.

ANGLE PAY PHONE

Gwen enters the booth and picks up the receiver. The WIRE HAS BEEN CUT. Desperate, she drops the receiver and runs from the booth.

ANGLE DOCK as Gwen passes various boats. She looks around for anything that can protect her, going through several fishing tools until she decides on a FISH GUTTING KNIFE.

GWEN (cont'd) Hello! Please, anybody!

The area resembles a ghost town - Gwen hurries further down the docks.

GWEN (cont'd) (slowing for a moment)

Gretchen.

Gwen hurries off in the direction of Gretchen's home.

CUT TO:

75. EXT. GRETCHEN'S HOUSEBOAT - NIGHT 75

Gwen, clutching her knife, hurries up to Gretchen's door and BANGS on it.

GWEN

Gretchen, it's Gwen - Gwen Newman. Gretchen?

Gwen tries the door, it's unlocked - she enters.

76. INT. TRAILER - CONTINUOUS- NIGHT76

C.U. Gwen as she enters, reacting with awe and worry as to what she sees.

ANGLE GWEN's P.O.V. - through the jungle of junk and stacks of newspapers, the WALL OF CLIPPINGS is now orderly. All of Horton's clips are perfectly symmetrical - like a Horton shrine.

Gwen steps into the shot, examining the new arrangement (SET DECORATOR NOTE: the difference must be immediately apparent).

GWEN

Oh my god ... Jack's been here.

O.C. the front door closes. Gwen spins with a GASP. ANGLE TO REVEAL Jack.

JACK

Correction. Jack *is* here.

Terrified, Gwen raises her large knife. Jack holds up his EVEN LARGER KNIFE.

JACK (cont'd) Mine's bigger than yours.

GWEN

You stay away from me, Jack.

Without taking her eyes off of Jack, Gwen backs up. He steps forward, taunting her.

GWEN (cont'd)

Don't you come near me - I'm not afraid to use this.

JΛCK

(smiling)

You're afraid of everything, Gwen.

GWEN

Jack, please ...

JACK

Listen to me, Gwen - Listen carefully ...

(with drama)

<u>Boo!</u>

Gwen gasps, then turns and runs deeper into the trailer.

77. INT. DEEPER IN HOUSEBOAT - CONTINUOUS 77

The "décor" gets worse the further in we go. Clutter and

filth add to the claustrophobia. Gwen desperately searches for a way out. She finds a door. She fumbles with the handle and yanks it open, revealing a closet. Inside is Gretchen, dead, hung on a hook. Her nose has been cut from her face. (LOCK DOWN SHOT NEEDED FOR POST EFFECT TO REMOVE NOSE, IF ACTRESS REFUSES TO REMOVE HER OWN NOSE). Gwen SCREAMS.

Jack appears at the top of the hall. In his hand he holds GRETCHEN'S NOSE.

JACK

She was such a nosy woman. But not anymore.

Gwen backs up against the closet wall. She tries to avoid Gretchen's dead body.

GWEN

(trembling)

Jack, please, don't ...

JACK

I've always been very particular about which body part I would collect. It was easy with her. It was easy with Sam - but I'm torn with you - you're a complicated woman, Gwendolyn. Which do I take - your heart ... or your brain?

Gwen pulls the door shut, putting a barrier between her and Jack. Now, Gwen is pressed up against dead Gretchen, her breathing rapid (Gwen, not Gretchen) - adrenaline pumping.

JACK'S VOICE

Let's not waste my time. I know what I want, now. You're clever, Gwen - I want your brain.

GWEN

Stay away, Jack, I swear I'll use this knife.

ANGLE - OUTSIDE CLOSET DOOR

Jack caresses the door for a moment until he yanks it open, revealing Gretchen. He is momentarily surprised. Gwen is gone.

JACK

(impressed)

Oh, Gwen, you ARE a clever one.

78. EXT. HOUSEBOAT - ANGLE OUTSIDE - NIGHT 78

Gwen frantically crawls through slime and mud near the docks, still wielding a knife.

ANGLE OUTSIDE TRAILER

Gwen emerges, caked with mud. She presses her back against the houseboat, searching for a direction to run.

ANGLE HOUSEBOATDOOR - SECONDS LATER

C.U. - front door swings open. Jack steps out and surveys the dock. He descends the steps, leans down and looks under around the trailer. Gwen's muddy footprints lead into the grass. He smiles.

JACK (CALLING OUT)

You can't get away, Gwen - no one's going to help you. They're all on the other side of the island -

(with a smile)

- digging up bodies. Jack rises, gripping his knife.

JACK (cont'd)

It's just you and me, baby. The honeymoon's over.

Jack walks off in the direction of Gwen's footprints. FRESH ANGLE FROM ABOVE

Gwen lies on the floor of a SMALL WOODEN BOAT, watching as Jack disappears into the foliage. She rolls on her back, relieved - for the moment.

DISSOLVE TO:

79. SAME LOCATION - NIGHT 79

Gwen hides in a small boat docked near Gretchen's house.- it is dark. She looks in all directions, then, under the cover of darkness, slips out of the boat, down onto the dock. (The mud on her clothes is now dried dirt).

Gwen creeps into the woods, the same direction Jack went, toward the lodge.

CUT TO:

80. EXT. OLD DOCKS - NIGHT 80

Lights are on a few of the boats. Gwen hurries toward them.

GWEN

Thank god.

Gwen runs to the first boat.

GWEN (cont'd)

Hello! Somebody, please help me!

No response. Gwen turns to move to the next boat and comes face to face with the Sheriff.

Gwen GASPS, but is quickly relieved to see that it is the Sheriff and not Jack.

GWEN (cont'd) Oh, Sheriff ...

The Sheriff sees the knife Gwen holds and steps back.

SHERIFF

I've been looking for you - you and that husband of yours. I have a few questions for him about the Congressman's wife ...

GWEN

He's not my husband ... I know it sounds crazy, but he's somebody else ... he's that killer, Terrence Lee Horton ...

A dark look crosses the Sheriff's face.

SHERIFF

I saw you talking to Gretchen - did she put this nonsense in your mind?

GWEN

She's dead! He killed her. She's back at the trailer. Horton killed a man, too - a doctor ... Sam Rieland ... his body's in the house where we were staying ...

SHERIFF

I've been to that house ... lookin' for you and your husband. There ain't no body there.

GWEN

It was! Jack cut his eyes out and put them in a martini glass.

Gwen bites off her words, realizing how crazy she must sound. The Sheriff holds out his hand.

SHERIFF

Give me the knife.

Gwen takes a step back.

GWEN

No.

SHERIFF

(annoyed)

Lady, I don't know what's going on in your head. I don't know what's going on in your marriage, either. But we've had one hell of a day out here, and I'm not much in the mood for any more of this.

Jack rises up behind the Sheriff. Jack reaches around and slashes his throat. The Sheriff's look of skepticism changes to one of horror and surprise. He clutches his throat, trying to speak. Gwen watches, horrified, as blood gushes from between his fingers. And then he drops out of frame, leaving her face to face with Jack.

JACK

Here we are, Gwen, the way you wanted it - just you and me, baby.

Gwen shakes her head. Jack backs her against a wall. She swipes the knife, trying to cut him, but he effortlessly knocks it out of her hand, keeping the bigger knife for himself.

JACK (cont'd)

You seem to be confused about something, Gwen. You told the Sheriff I'm Horton. I'm not Horton

- I'm Jack.

Gwen tries to run past Jack. He flings her back against the railing.

JACK (cont'd)

You know I've always been fascinated with evil - I discuss it with my students - what makes a person do horrible dark things?

Gwen again tries to get away. Jack again shoves her back.

JACK (cont'd)

Somehow ... since the operation, I've been ... enlightened. I can see what Horton saw - those horrible things he did. I suppose his eyes have helped me understand

... evil.

Gwen lashes out at Jack, swinging at him. He throws her to the dock, then straddles her, pinning her arms down.

JACK (cont'd)

I want to put this thought in your head before I take your brain.

It'll make it all the more special. (leans in; intimately)

I've learned from Horton that we all have evil within, all of us - it's inside you too.

GWEN

No it's not!

JACK

Yes, Gwen, even you. But as we're civilized, social creatures, we've been taught to control our primal instincts.

(MORE)

JACK (cont'd)

We just can't go around bashing each others heads in, now, can we?

GWEN

(sobbing) Jack, please...

JACK

Listen to me, this is important. When we put restraints on our own personal evil, we're not truly free. And, if we are not truly free, we are not truly alive.

Gwen tries to shift away, whimpering. Jack turns her face to his.

JACK (cont'd)

For those who suppress evil, the only freedom they have to look forward to in life ... is in death.

(leans closer)

My gift to you, darling, is your freedom.

Jack presses his knife against Gwen's forehead, precisely where her brain is.

Terrified, Gwen struggles and manages to fold her leg between her and Jack. With her foot she throws Jack back.

Jack GASPS.

FRESH ANGLE REVEALS JACK IMPALED ON A POLE/RIGGING/MAST.

Gwen reacts in horror.

Jack, still "Evil Jack," tries to move but he is paralyzed below the arms. He looks down at the bloodied skewer protruding from his chest.

JACK (cont'd)

Oh...

Jack looks at Gwen. The evil seems to drain from his face, returning to "Good Jack."

Gwen stands and takes an apprehensive step toward him.

JACK (cont'd) (relieved)

Gwen ... thank god you're safe.

As Gwen stares at Jack, her eyes well with tears.

GWEN

You're free now baby.

Jack slowly reaches out to touch Gwen's face like he did with the facial expression of Gwen in the beginning of our story.

JACK

When you're upset...this muscle tighten more...than the other...

As Jacks words trail off Gwen puts both hands on his face as she struggles to get the slightest word out, her face filled with tears.

GWEN

Jack.

Jack smiles, holding his gaze until his eyes slowly go dead.

Emotionally drained, Gwen slides her trembling body down to her knees. She tries to sooth herself by rocking.

CAMERA SLOWLY PULLS BACK to include Gwen, rocking, Jack, impelled and dead, and the Sheriff's lifeless body.

DISSOLVE TO:

81. EXT. OLD DOCKS-EARLY MORNING 81

We PUSH IN to Gwen, face frozen in shock as she stares at the calm water. A beam of early morning sunlight finally breaks her daydreaming.

82. EXT. OLD DOCK-LATER 82

As several Sheriff Deputy's investigate the murder scene we see one of the officers walk over to Gwen and wrap a BLANKET around a freezing Gwen. After a moment she returns her sight to the water. C.U. Of river.

GWEN (V.O.)

... so we can see that the nature of evil is not something as clearly defined as we might think. For some, evil will be an abstract battle, a notional debate about the actions of man ...

DISSOLVE TO:

83. INT. CLASSROOM - DAY 83

SUPER: “Eight months later”

CAMERA MOVES past the students to see Gwen lecturing a class. She is very PREGNANT.

GWEN

So, consider this: is evil born, bred, nurtured or simply the work of the “devil?”

Gwen seems to speak as much to herself as the class.

GWEN (cont’d)

For others it is more personal. Evil is ...

The CAMERA moves in on Gwen.

GWEN (cont’d)

- A very personal thing.

CLOSER

GWEN (cont’d)

- A very real thing.

CAMERA pushes in to PICTURE OF JACK AND GWEN on the desk as we:

FADE OUT.

We fade to black for a few moments until we:

FADE UP:

84. EXT. CAMPUS - DUSK84

SUPER: "Six months later".

Gwen sits on A BENCH trying to enjoy a beautiful day on the University grounds. After a few moments the BABY begins to cry.

Gwen turns her attention to her baby.

GWEN

Hush, hush, little one - Daddy and I love you.

(beat)

He's watching...

Obediently the crying stops.

C.U. Baby - he has one blue eye and one brown (LOCK DOWN, POST FX).

GWEN (O.C.) (cont'd)

... he's always watching.

CUT TO BLACK.

PART 4

The Making of In the Eyes of a Killer

Production Steps

Cast & Crew

Call Sheets

Props

Work Days

Equipment

Sound

Wardrobe

Development
(ten weeks)

First draft of screenplay
Script Breakdown
Determine Project Budget
Secure Entertainment Attorney
Secure Entertainment Accountant
Active search for Sales Agent
Set up production office
Set up production accounts
Secure Insurance/Bonds
Begin casting
Active search for a Composer
Active search for an Editor

- Location scouting
- Active search for Distribution
- LLC Incorporation
- Marketing & PR (brochures, bus. Cards, website)
- Market Research
- Finalize Investment Memorandum
- Lock production schedule
- Active Search for Department heads
  - Gaffer
  - Production Designer
  - Sound
  - Wardrobe & Make-up Designers

Pre-Production
Upon receiving funding
(four weeks)

Finalize and secure Cast
Rehearsals
Secure department heads
Secure Director's team
- Assistant Director(s), etc.

Sign contracts and release scripts
Secure locations
Any necessary re-writes
Individual departments will begin and complete:

- Securing crews
- Building sets
- Design/locate/create wardrobe
- Design/locate/create sets & properties
- Arrange travel and lodging
- Conduct camera tests
- Wardrobe and make-up test, etc
- Secure Composer
- Secure Editor

Production
(three-weeks)

Principal photography begins
Time line (include. travl/set up time betwn loc.)

- Begin editing
- Begin scoring

Post-Production
(ten to twelve weeks) [which begins first day of filming)

Editing
Scoring
Sound mix foley
Looping

- Titles
- Re-shoots
- Screenings
- Final prints for distribution

SUMMARY PRODUCTION COSTS

PRODUCTION NUMBER TITLE DATE

PRODUCER ASSOCIATE PRODUCER DIRECTOR

CAST WRITER CAMERAMAN

DATE STARTED SCHEDULED FINISH DATE FINISH DATE

ACCT. No.	CLASSIFICATION	BUDGET	COST TO DATE	ESTIMATED COST TO COMPLETE	ESTIMATED TOTAL COST	OVER OR (UNDER) BUDGET
01	Story					
02	Supervisors					
03	Cast					
04	Direction					
Total Above the Line Costs						
05	Director's Staff /D.P.					
06	Camera /GRIP/ELECTRICAL					
07	Set Operations /CREW					
08	Set Construction Cost					
09	Set Design					
10	Set Dressings					
11	Special Effects					
12	Process					
13	Miniature /MEALS					
14	Draperies / INSURANCE					
15	Props					
16	Live Stock — Handlers and Eqpt.					
17	Locations					
18	Transportation					
19	Lighting					
20	Wardrobe					
21	Make-up and Hairdressing					
22	Film and Laboratory					
23	Sound Recording / SHOOT					
24	Sound Royalties / XFERS					
25	Sound Dubbing and Scoring/RE-RCDNG					
26	Film Editing					
27	Titles and Inserts					
28	Music					
29	Studio Rentals					
30	Tests and Pre-production /NGTV CTTNG					
31	Studio General /OFFICE					
Total Below the Line Costs						
Total Direct Cost						
40 - 000	Contingency					
50	General Studio Overhead					
TOTAL COST						

Remarks:

Film Budgeted Feet Film Shot Feet

Signed Signed

Producer Production Dept.

FIGURE 1
RATE OF RETURN

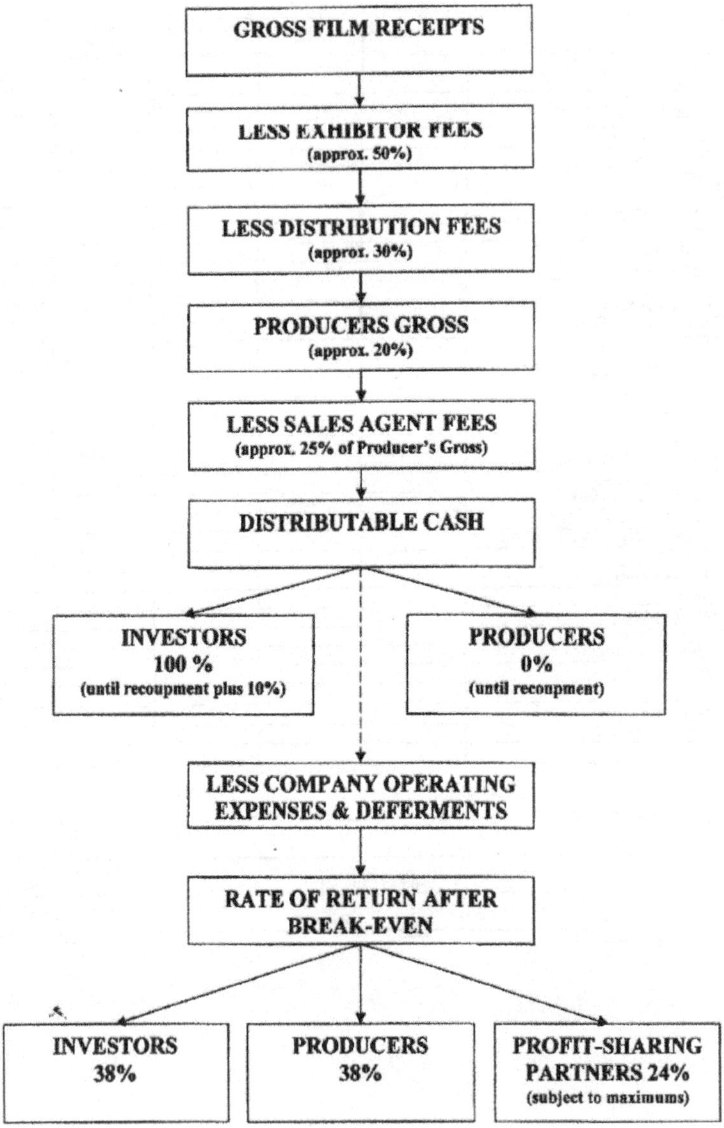

PART 5

Cast

LOUIS MANDYLOR

Director of In The Eyes of a Killer

Starring as Jack

COSTAS MANDYLOR

as Congressman Donaldson

GWENDOLYN EDWARDS

as Gwen

JAMES MARSHALL

as The Sheriff

RANDY COLTEN

as Dr. Reiland

SHERRY WESTON

as Gretchen

PETRI HAWKINS-BYRD

as Clarence

SHAUNA HARRINGTON

as Karl

Nick Fenske, an acclaimed actor with a myriad of achievements, takes a chilling turn in Mamie Jean Calvert's psychological thriller, *In the Eyes of a Killer*, portraying the enigmatic serial killer Terrence Lee Horton. Despite facing stiff competition during auditions, Fenske emerged victorious, securing the role with unparalleled skill and conviction.

Delving into the psyche of a serial killer proved to be an unforgettable experience for Fenske, who acknowledges the challenge of immersing himself in such dark territory. In a candid statement, he reflected on the demanding role, expressing that playing a character like Terrence Lee Horton requires delving deep into the killer's mind, an endeavor that leaves a lasting impact on both the actor and the audience.

Fenske, in an interview, shared his perspective on the audience's reaction to his portrayal, stating, "The best thing an actor can hear is, 'You are going to give me nightmares.' This means I have done my job as an actor." Revealing the gratification derived from portraying Terrence Lee Horton, he emphasized the delicate balance between captivating the audience and leaving a lasting, haunting impression.

Around the set, Fenske became synonymous with the character, playfully adopting the name "Horty." His exceptional performance as the notorious serial killer adds another feather to his illustrious cap, showcasing his versatility and mastery in bringing complex characters to life on the silver screen.

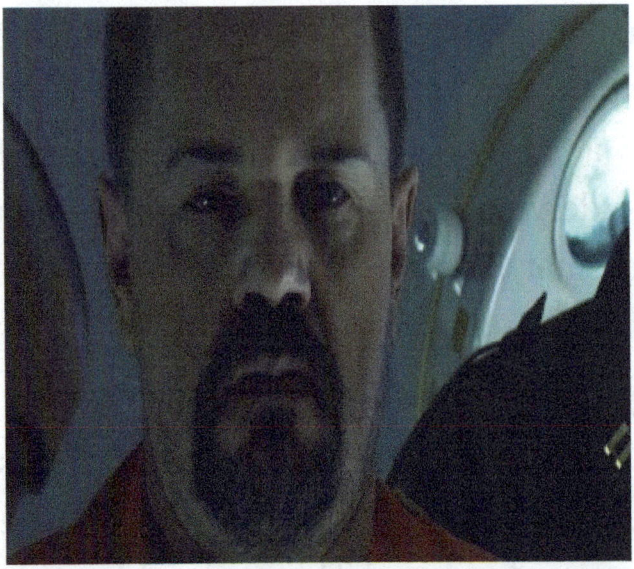

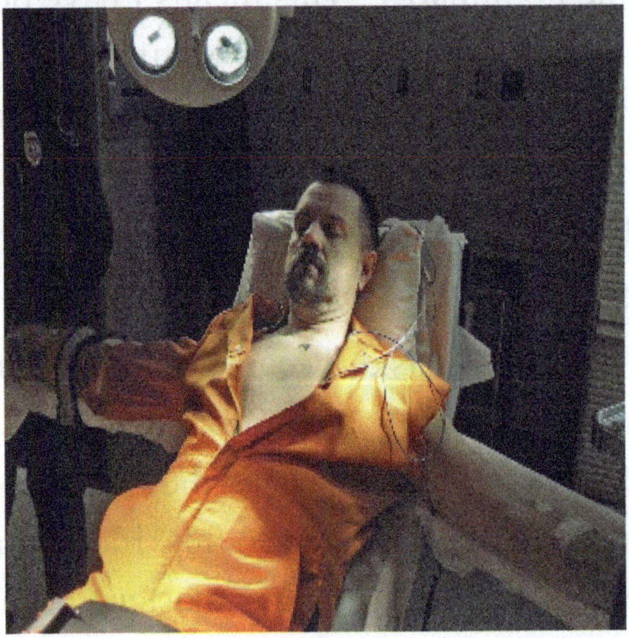

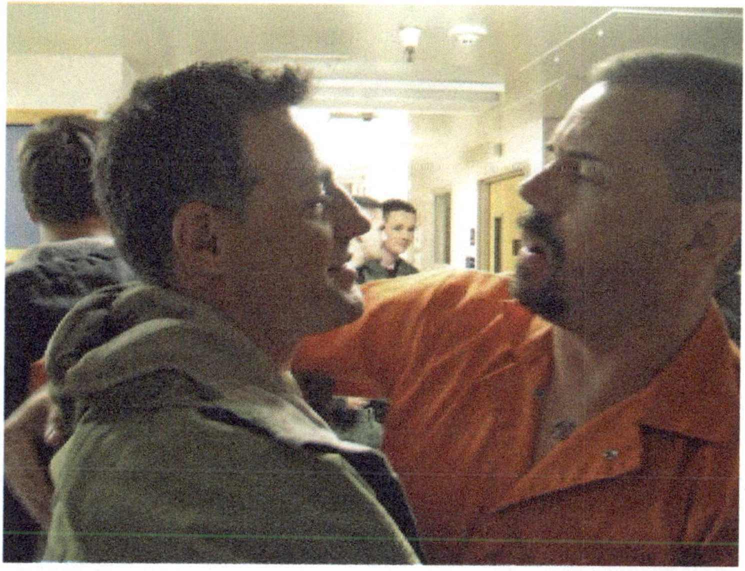

PART 6

Cast & Crew

DIRECTED BY – Louis Mandylor

SCREENPLAY – Mamie Jean Calvert

ADDITIONAL DIALOGUE – Marc Cushman

SOME ADDITIONAL DIALOGUE – Josh Porter

TYPIST – Susan Osborn

STORY BY – Mamie Jean Calvert

CAST

Louis Mandylor – Jack

Gwendolyn Edwards – Gwen

James Marshall – The Sheriff

Costas Mandylor – Congressman Donaldson

Randy Colton – Dr. Rieland

Petri Hawkins Byrd – Clarence

Sherry Weston – Gretchen

Shauna Harrington – Kari

Tyler Cook – Bobby

Jeff Redlick – Warden

Nick Fenske – Special thanks to Nick Fenske who played our serial killer and did a lot of research to get into the head of how a killer would react.

ADDITIONAL CAST

Rick Pulido – Mr. Bigler

Valerie Cortopassi – Sally

Bob Krull – Priest

Tris Rieland – Doctor

Tamara Chandler – Attending Nurse

Lisa Lee Smith – Girl in Restaurant

Thomas Perry – Guard

John K. Cortesi – Guard

Matt Carroll – Guard

Darren Ross – Guard

Robert Edward Thomas – Deputy James Harris

Darcel M. Douglas – CPA MS Taxation

Rick Camp – Dock Master

Witt Widmer – Boat Wrangler

Ron Bonomo – Earl (Louis's stand in)

Jessie Harris – Dell

Jessica McNally – Girl in tub

Holly Sherman – Girlfriend

Randi Cowley – Scrub Nurse

Oscar Russell – Anesthesiologist

Ken Bledvins – Lethal Injection Technician

Mark Smith – Elvis Impersonator

Rebecca Washo – B-Movie

Kelly Symone – (as Kelly Stringfellow) Reporter (Costas Mandylor's Driver)

Frank Babcock – Reporter

Ambra Battiato – Mother of Child Star/Reporter

Jeff Nessen – Reporter

Penny Van Saint – Family

Lori Beausheur – Family

Todd Arslenia – Family

Dianna Apodaca – Family

Marie Crocket – Family

Doug Wright – Family

Tris Rieland – Doctor

Oscar Russell – Anesthesiologist

Randi Cowley – Scrub Nurse

Keenan Johnston – Restaurant Patron

Nicoli Pineda – The Baby

Ken Bledvins – Anesthesiologist

Zairma Patel – Girl on Yacht

John Douglas Ayers – B-Movie Killer

Al Cacioppo – News Cameraman

Robert Granados – Rock Creek

Mamie Jean Calvert – Mrs. Bigler (as Mamie Jean)

Max – The Dog

Ryan Nelson – Student

Erik Dorn – Student

Jeffery T. Ferguson – Boat Passenger (as Jeff Ferguson)

Doug Wright – Family Member

IN THE EYES OF A KILLER – PRODUCED BY AMBRA PRODUCTIONS LLC with KRAKATAU FILM

CREW

Producers

Executive Producer – Robert T. Calvert

Executive Producer – Mamie Jean

Executive Producer – Witt Widmer

Executive Producer – Tris Rieland

Executive Producer – Jacqueline C. Rieland

Executive Producer – Carolyn Munson

Executive Producer – Jo Hoffmeir

Executive Producer – Judy Nessen

Executive Producer – Linda Ramsey

Executive Producer – Faye Krull

Producer – Mamie Jean

Producer – Louis Mandylor

Co-Producer – Al Cacioppo

Co-Producer – Joel A. Fox

Associate Producer – Linda Arslanian

Associate Producer – Jeff Redlick

Associate Producer – Nick Fenske

Composer

Music by Deane Ogden

Distribution

Distribution – Odyssey Motion Pictures, Marc Clebanoff

Distribution – Pamela Vlasatas

Cinematographer

Cinematography by Ted Caloroso

Editor

Editing by Russell White

Casting Directors

Casting by Mamie Jean Calvert and Eileen O'Farrell

Production Design

Production Design by Janene White

Costume Department

Costume Design and Wardrobe by Tamara Chandler

Makeup Department

Key Makeup – Barbara McGee

Special Effects Makeup – John Douglas Ayers

Assistant Special Effects Makeup – Jen William

Production Manager

Production Manager – Charlene Blanco Agabao

Assistant Director

Second Unit Director – Serenity Pang

First Assistant Director – Serenity Xiao Xiao Pang – Bellman

Sound Department

Sound mixer/Supervising sound editor – Houston Haynes

Boom Operator – Jon Vennarucci

Production Sound Mixer – Nikolas Zasimczuk

Camera and Electrical Department

Assistant Camera – Amy Olk

Electrician – Benjamin Casias

Electrician – Keenan Johnston

Electrician – Drew Nelson

Electrician – Rod Betamoza

Key Grip – Ryan Baustian

Grip – Jeff Smith

Best Boy – Samuel Kim

Best Boy Electric – Russell Smith

Behind the Scenes Camera – Al Cacioppo

Gaffer – Nghia Khuu

Gaffer – Michael Schilling

Gaffer – Jeff Smith

Editorial Department

Colorist – Ran Ballard

Music Department

Music Preparation – Mark Estes

Score Mixer – Tom Geron

Orchestrator – Deane Ogden

Assistant to Composer – Jai Meghan

Original Song "Delta Breeze" Written By Mamie Jean

Continuity Department

Script Supervisor – Judy Nessen

Additional Crew Members

Stuntman – John Douglas

Transportation Coordinator – Debra Battiato

Chef – Tony Retto

Craft Service – Jack Sorono

Story Consultant – Robert Edwards Thomas

Production Assistant – Jeff Smith

Production Assistant – Tony Randolph

Production Assistant – David Ferraro

Attorney at Law – Richard A. Proaps

Entertainment Attorney – Christine Lynn O'Connor

Public Relations – Leslie Paris

Book Design – Sierra Bogusz

Special Thanks

Ambra Battiato

Lisa Randolph

Carla Giampapa

Dylan Bogusz

Todd Arslanian

Jeff Nessen

Karyn Yarris

Jason Bortz

Marie Crocket

Penny Van Saint

Sheila Campbell

Kathy Campbell

Martin Anaya

Debra Jean Battiato

Lisa Lee Smith

Damien Rivelli

PART 7

Behind The Scenes

Day to Day Notes

Nov. 12:
26 - bungalow entrance/ living room
Jack and Gwen first see bungalow and kiss
38 - bungalow, poolside
Jack wakes up with hangover, fights w/ Gwen, leaves
42 - Jacks POV from speedboat
Gwen storms back into bungalow
52 - bungalow living rm
Jack returns from fishing, fight w/ Gwen, storms off
30 - docks
Jack is drunk, singing, walking back to bungalow w/ Gwen
71 - bungalow entrance, EXT
Gwen returns from Gretchen's
74 - bungalow entrance, EXT
Gwen sees Sam dead, runs off
72 - bungalow entrance, INT
Gwen returns from Gretchen's, notices Sam's bag

Nov. 13:
62 - bungalow entrance
Sam enters
63 - bungalow living rm
Sam meets Jack
64 - bungalow bedrm
Sam hides, grabs lamp
65 - bungalow hallway
Jack looks for Sam
66 - bungalow bedrm
Jack attacks Sam
73 - bungalow bar
Gwen returns, sees Sam dead

Nov. 14:
41 - speedboat
Jack cruises around
43 - speedboat
Jack heads to trail
44 - north shore trail
Jack ties up boat
40 - old dock
Jack rents boat from Grady
61 - old dock
Sam arrives, sees Earl and Dell
19 - dream sequence - woodpile - ext

Horton POV, kills Gwen
60 - dream sequence - woodpile - N
Horton kills Gwen, has no eyes, turns into Jack
6 - trees - ext
b-movie scene

Nov. 15:
45 - north trail
Jack meets Bigler, scares him away
35 - north trail
Jack and Gwen frolic
36 - north trail
Jack and Gwen picnic and talk
COMPANY MOVE
39 - Congressman Donalds' yacht --> OMIT?
Kari flirts w/ Jack, gets caught by Donalds
51 - Congressman Donalds' yacht - INT -->N?
Kari dances for Donald, Jack watches
56 - Congressman Donalds' yacht - EXT
Jack kills Kari

Nov. 16:
34 - bungalow living rm - table
Jack and Gwen have sex
57 - bungalow living rm
Jack slaps, threatens Gwen
58 - bungalow poolside
Jack falls into pool, Gwen rescues him, Jack confesses he killed Kari

Nov. 17:
28 - bungalow bath rm - flash
Horton POV of killing Victim #1 in shower
59 - bungalow bathroom/bedroom
Gwen, naked in shower, cries and watches Jack, who has nightmares
31 - bungalow bathroom/bedroom
Gwen, in lingerie, sits on bed; Jack pukes in bathroom
32 - bungalow bathroom
Jack notices tile, has flashback, blood runs down drain
33 - bungalow bedrm
clock says - 3:15am, jack spoons Gwen
11 - Jack's house - bedrm - int - n
Jack and Gwen make love

Nov. 20:
68 - north shore trail
Sheriff finds body (Gretchen, Gwen, Bigler, Mamie, Clarence, Deputy + Extras)

COMPANY MOVE
37 - restaurant
Jack and Gwen drink w/ Kari and Donalds, and Sheriff. Gretchen serves them.
24 - arriving dock
Jack POV looking at Sheriff

Nov. 21:
67 - old dock
Sheriff finds Kari's body. (Donalds, Earl, Dell, Bobby, Deputy, Clarence, Gretchen, Gwen)
80 - old dock
Jack chases Gwen, kills Sheriff
81 - old dock
Jack dies, Gwen is in shock
82 - old dock
Deputy arrives, puts blanket on Gwen

Nov. 24:
4 - university campus - ext
Jack and Gwen stroll and talk
83 - university campus - int
Gwen, pregnant, lectures students
22 - university classroom - int
Gwen finishes class, Jack visits (students leaving)
21 - university campus - b-roll
estb. shot
3 - university classrm
Jack practices lecture, Gwen walks in

Nov. 25:
5 - Sally's house - patio - ext
Sally and Gwen talk
46 - docks - phone booth -ext
Gwen walks to phone booth to make a call
47 - docks - phone booth - ext
Gwen talks to Sam (on phone) sees Mika gut a fish
48 - docks - phone booth
Gwen calls Sam, Jack on speedboat, passes by
50 - docks - phone booth
Gwen finishes call, Mika chops fish head
54 - docks - phone booth - N
Gwen calls Sam, crying
55 - docks - phone booth - N
Gwen talks to Sam
74A - docks -phone booth N
Gwen sees phone line is cut, tries to wave to Dell and Earl for help, grabs fish-gutting

knife <--- OMIT?

Nov. 26:
23 - Ferry
Jack and Gwen meet Bobby, Jack observes Gretchen (Bigler, Mamie, bits, extras)
24A- arriving dock
All arrive, greeted by Clarence
COMPANY MOVE
27 - Restaurant
Jack and Gwen are waited on by Bobby
29 - restaurant
Jack knocks over plate, everyone stares at him (gretchen, mamie, bigler, kari, donalds)
53 - restaurant
Jack drinks with Donalds, Kari; Gretchen bartends

Nov. 27:
69 - gretchen boathouse - ext
gwen and gretchen enter boat house
70 - gretch boathse - int
gretchen shows gwen horton murder clippings
75 - gretchen boathse - ext - N
gwen enters boathouse w/knife
76 -gretchen boathse - int - N
gwen notices re-arranged murder clippings, Jack appears
77 - gretchen boathse -int - a room - N
Gwen finds Gretchen's body, tries to run away from Jack
78 - gretchen's boathse - hiding spot - ext - N
Gwen hides, jack tries to find her
79 - gretchen's boathse -hiding spot - ext - N
Gwen runs away

Nov. 28:
12 - dr. sam office - int
Jack and Gwen visit Sam
47A - dr. sam office - int
Gwen calls, Sam picks up phone
48A - Dr. sam office -int
Sam talks to Gwen; insert magazine with Sam on cover
49 - dr. sam office int - d
Sam talks to Gwen on phone
55A - dr. sam office - int -n
Sam talks to Gwen on phone, has Horton's pic
1 - prison hallway -int -n
guards walk with horton ---> OMIT
2 - execution room/ viewing room - int - n
Horton is executed, victims' families watch (doctor, warden, guards, reporters)

Nov. 29:
84 - jack's house - ext
gwen talks to baby
20 - jack's house -backyard -ext - d
Jack and Gwen celebrate with champagne
7 - Jack's house - kitchen - int - n
Jack cooks dinner with b-movie playing
8 - Jack's house - dining rm - int. n
Gwen brings in groceries and flowers
9 - Jack's house - kitchen -int - n
Jack cooks, Gwen enters, turns off b-movie, leaves; Jack turns b-movie back on.
10 - Jack's house - dining rm - int
Jack and have dinner, Jack gives Gwen gift
14 - Jack's house - kitchen - int - n
Jack accidentally destroys gift

Dec. 2:
13 - dr. sam office - ext - d
Jack almost gets hit by car, Gwen runs in to help him
16 - hospital - rm - int - d
Sam, Gwen, Reporters all check on Jack, post-op
17 - hospital - rm - int - d
Sam, Gwen, Reporters all watch when Jack's bandages are removed
18 - hospital - rm -n
Jack has nightmares
15 - hospital -op room - in - n
Sam and Medical Staff perform surgery; Reporters watch

SCENE 1

CH: Horton, Guard #1, Guard #2

Location: Prison Corridor, EXT, NIGHT

Production Design: Prison Corridor

Props: Handcuffs, footlocks, Horton's blue/brown contacts, guard's props, keys

Wardrobe: Horton's orange suit, guard's uniforms

Make Up: Horton

Notes:

SCENE 2

CH: Horton, Guard #1, #2, Warden, Prison Doctor, Victim's Family, Reporters, Prison officials, Sketch artist

L: Execution Room/ Press Room INT, NIGHT

PD: Metal table w/ straps and chains, chairs, viewing mirror, wall clock, black viewing curtain

P: Handcuffs, footlocks, Horton's contacts, guard's props, Keys, sketch pad, pencil, swab cotton, canula injection w/ tube, pocket watch, stethoscope

W: Horton's orange suit, guard's uniforms, warden's suit, doctor's coat, prison officials's uniforms, family members.

MK: Horton, Horton's tattoo Warden

N: Extras, Horton's tattoo

SCENE 3

CH: Jack, Gwen

L: University classroom, INT, DAY

PD: Classroom, teaching table, blackboard w/ notes on, chairs

P: Books, pens, Jack's cane

W: Jack1 and Gwen1

MK: Jack1 and Gwen1

N:

SCENE 4

CH: Jack and Gwen

L: University campus, EXT, DAY

PD: U campus

P: Jack's cane,

W: Jack 1, Gwen 1

MK: Jack, Gwen

N:

SCENE 5
CH: Gwen, Sally
L: Sally's Patio, EXT, DAY
PD: Chairs, table
P: Candy bar , coffee cups
W: Gwen1, Sally
MK: Gwen1, Sally
N:

SCENE 6
CH: Killer, frightened woman
L: Tree lined area, EXT, NIGHT
PD: foggy?
P: Butcher knife (robber and real), fake blood
W: Killer, Frightened woman
MK: Killer, Frightened woman
N: Stunt, real knife, need that footage for scene 7 in the kitchen TV

SCENE 7
CH: Jack
L: Jack's house kitchen, INT, NIGHT
PD: neat and orderly Kitchen, small tv
P: big pot, sauce ingredient, spaghetti
W: Jack1
MK: Jack1
N: slasher film on

Scene 8
CH: Jack and Gwen
L: Jack's house dining room, INT, NIGHT
PD: perfectly set dinner table
P: Groceries, flowers
W: Gwen1
MK: Gwen1
N:

SCENE 9

CH: Jack, Gwen

L: Jack's house kitchen, INT, NIGHT

PD: Kitchen

P: sauce spoon, sauce in pot, other ingredient from SCN 7, groceries, flowers

W: Jack 1, Gwen 1

MK: Jack 1, Gwen 1

N: slasher film playing (when turns off and when turns back on)

SCENE 10

CH: Jack, Gwen

L: Jack's house dining room, INT, NIGHT

PD: Jack's dining room

P: remaining food, wine glasses, burnt candles, Gwen's gift

W: Jack 1, Gwen 1

MK: Jack1, Gwen 1

N: need 2 or more copies of Gwen's gift

SCENE 11

CH: Jack, Gwen

L: Jack's bedroom, INT, NIGHT

PD: Jack's bedroom, (record player?)

P: scarf

W: Jack1, Gwen 1 clothes somewhere in the bedroom

MK: Jack1, Gwen1

N: close set

SCENE 12

CH: Jack, Gwen, Dr. Sam

L: Dr. Sam's office, INT, DAY

PD: doctor's office

P: Jack's cane, eye diagram, desk calendar

W: Jack2, Gwen 2, Sam1

MK: Jack1, Gwen1

N:

SCENE 13

CH: Jack, Gwen, reporters, driver

L: Medical center, EXT, DAY

PD: Car

P: Jack's cane, reporter's mics, cameras, notepads

W: Jack2, Gwen2

MK: Jack1, Gwen1

N: stunt w/ car, extras

SCENE 14

CH: Jack, Gwen

L: Jack's House kitchen, INT, NIGHT

PD: Jack's kitchen

P: chopped vegetables, knife, jack's cane, wet cloth, fake blood, Gwen's gift

W: Jack2, Gwen2

MK:Jack1, Gwen1

N: cut hand

SCENE 15

CH: Jack, Sam, Assistant, medical staff, camera crew

L: Operation room, INT, DAY

PD: operation room

P: Eye Clamps, clock, Jack eyes, Horton's eyes in solution jar

W: Jack's patient gown, scrubs

MK:

N: 2 holes to set in the new eye, do we need jack in the scene?

SCENE 16

CH: Jack, Gwen, Sam, Reporters

L: Hospital room, INT, DAY

PD: Hospital room

P: Bandage, notepads, cameras

W: Jack's patient's gown, Dr. Sam's coat, Gwen3

MK: Sam, Gwen1, Jack

N: extra

SCENE 17

CH: Jack, Gwen, Sam, Nurse, reporters, camera crew

L: Hospital room, INT, DAY

PD: Hospital room

P: Jack's contacts, solution, bandage, camera

W: Jack's gown,Gwen4, Dr's coat, Nurse uniform

MK: Gwen1, sam, Jack1

N: extra

SCENE 18

CH: Jack

L: Hospital room, INT, NIGHT

PD: Hospital room

W: Jack's P gown

MK:

N: Light off

SCENE 19

CH: Horton(double), Gwen

L: Wood wall area, EXT, NIGHT

PD: Foggy

P:

W: Killer, Gwen(white dress?)

MK: Gwen

N: Killer POV, stunt

SCENE 20

CH: Jack, Gwen

L: Jack's house backyard, EXT, DAY

PD: patio chairs

P: Bottle of champagne, glasses, Jack's sunglasses, Jack's contacts

W: Jack3, Gwen5

MK: Jack1,Gwen1

N: champagne level

SCENE 21

Campus Establish Shot

SCENE 22

CH: Gwen, Jack, students

L: University classroom

PD: Gwen's class, teacher table, chairs

P: Jack's glasses, travel brochures, lighthouse resort photos, Books, school bags, pens

W: Gwen6, Jack4

MK: Gwen1, Jack1

N: extras

SCENE 23

CH: Jack, Gwen, Bobby, Bigler, Mamie, Gretchen, 6 passengers, ferry crew

L: Arriving ferry, EXT, DAY

PD:

P: Jack's sunglasses, Jack's contacts, Gretchen's book, Bigler's metal detector

W: Jack5, Gwen7, Bobby's boots, Bigler, Mamie, Gretchen

MK: Jack1, Gwen1

N: Extras, Gretchen's book title, same shot as the resort brochure

SCENE 24

CH: Jack, Gwen, Clarence, Bobby, Bigler, Mamie, Gretchen, 6 passengers, ferry crew

L: Arriving dock, EXT, DAY

PD:

P: Jack's sunglasses, Jack's contacts, Gretchen's book, Bigler's metal detector

W: Jack5, Gwen7, Bobby's boots, Bigler, Mamie, Gretchen, Clarence, MK: Jack1, Gwen1

N: We don't see Sheriff in this scene, Extras

SCENE 24A

CH: Sheriff

L: Arriving dock*,EXT,DAY

PD:

P: Sheriff's prop

W: Sheriff's uniform

MK: Sheriff

N: Just Insert for Sheriff, will shot this outside the restaurant

SCENE 25

Bungalow Establish shot

SCENE 26

CH: Jack, Gwen

L: Bungalow, INT, DAY

PD: Record players

P: LDs

W: Jack5, Gwen7

MK: Jack1, Gwen1

N:

SCENE 27

CH: Jack, Gwen, Bobby, Gretchen, Ed, Kari, Bigler, Mamie, extras

L: Restaurant Patio, EXT/INT, NIGHT

PD: Restaurant patio lights

P: Whiskey on rock, wine, Jack's contacts

W: Jack5, Gwen7, Ed, Kari, Gretchen, Bobby(waiter)

MK: Jack1, Gwen1, Ed, Kari, Gretchen, Bobby

N: shoot w/ scene 29, boats w/ lights in the background, Extras

SCENE 28

CH: Horton (double), Victim#1

L: Shower, INT, NIGHT

PD: Shower, shower curtain (2), decal tile

P: knife, fake blood

W: Horton's double

MK:

N: FX makeup for peeling hair off scalp, close set, stunt

SCENE 29

CH: Jack, Gwen, Bobby, Gretchen, Ed, Kari, Bigler, Mamie, extras

L: Restaurant Patio, EXT/INT, NIGHT

PD: Restaurant patio lights

P: Whiskey on rock, wine, Jack's contacts, plate of food, knock down plate of food(extra food to make more plates)

W: Jack5, Gwen7, Ed, Kari, Gretchen, Bobby(waiter)

MK: Jack1, Gwen1, Ed, Kari, Gretchen, Bobby

N: shoot w/ scene 29, boats w/ lights in the background, Extras

SCENE 30
CH: Jack, Gwen
L: Dock outside Bungalow, EXT, N
PD:
P: Jack's contacts
W: Jack5, Gwen7,
MK: Jack1, Gwen1
N:

SCENE 31
CH: Gwen, Jack(o.s)
L: Bungalow Bedroom/bathroom, INT, NIGHT
PD: Bungalow bedroom
P: Champagne, glasses
W: Sexy negligee-Gwen
MK: Gwen1
N: Jack puking in the background, close set

SCENE 32
CH: Jack
L: BG Bathroom, INT,NIGHT
PD: Decal tile, shower curtain
P: vomit, fake blood
W: Jack5
MK: sick Jack
N: mirror reflection

SCENE 33
CH: Jack, Gwen
L: BG Bedroom, INT, NIGHT
PD: BG bedroom
P: Digital clock showing 3:15am
W:
MK:
N: Lights off

SCENE 34
CH: Jack, Gwen

L: BG Dining room
PD: Dining room set, table center piece (unbreakable)
P: Coffee, cups, Jack's sunglasses
W: robe? PJs
MK: morning
N: close set, sex scene

SCENE 35
CH: Jack, Gwen
L: Trail, EXT, DAY
PD: Distinctive tree area
P: Jack's sunglasses, Gwen's bag, blanket
W: Jack6, Gwen8
MK: Jack1, Gwen1
N: windy

SCENE 36
CH: Jack, Gwen
L: Trail Beach, EXT, DAY
PD:
P: Jack's sunglasses, Gwen's bag, blanket
W: Jack6, Gwen8
MK: Jack1, Gwen1
N: windy

SCENE 37
CH: Jack, Gwen, Sheriff, Gretchen, Ed, Kari, Extras
L: Light house restaurant, INT, DAY
PD: Restaurant/ bar
P: Jack's contacts, whiskey on rocks, wine, drinks, Kari's necklace
W: Jack7, Gwen9, Ed, Kari, sheriff's uniform, Gretchen
MK:Jack1, Gwen1
N: Extras, Eric hours, boats in background

SCENE 38
CH: Jack, Gwen
L: BG Poolside Patio, EXT, DAY
PD: Tables, chairs

P: Newspaper, coffee, Jack's sunglasses
W: Jack's robe, Gwen morning cloth
MK: Jack (hangover), Gwen morning mk
N:

SCENE 39
CH: Jack, Kari, ED
L: Ed's yacht , EXT, DAY
PD:
P: Jack's sunglasses, Kari's sunglasses, Kari's necklace
W: Jack8, Kari's bikini, Ed
MK: Jack2, Kari, Ed
N: Kari in bikini, provide warmth

SCENE 40
CH: Jack, Grady
L: Old dock, EXT,DAY
PD: Speedboat, cabinet
P: Jack's sunglasses, $75 bills, keys,
W: Jack8, Grady
MK: Jack2
N: need speedboat, limited crew on set, dangerous location

SCENE 41
CH: Jack
L: On speedboat on water, EXT, DAY
PD: speedboat
W: Jack8
P: Jack's sunglasses
MK: Jack2
N: camera and DP on boat, life jackets

SCENE 42
CH: Jack, Gwen
L: Speedboat, BG Patio, EXT, DAY
PD:

P: Jack's sunglasses, Gwen's sunglasses
W: Jack 8
MK: Jack 2, Gwen 2
N: 2 shots, one from Jack's POV, one from Gwen's POV

SCENE 43
CH: Jack
L: Speedboat, EXT, DAY
PD:
P: Jack's sunglasses
W: Jack 8
MK: Jack2
N: Going towards trail direction

SCENE 44
CH: Jack
L: North shore trail, EXT, DAY
PD: Speedboat tie on shore, distinctive tree area
P: Jack's sunglasses
W: Jack 8
MK: Jack 2
N:

SCENE 45
CH: Jack, Bigler
L: Trail, EXT, DAY
PD: distinctive tree area, dirt
P: Jack's sunglasses, jack's contacts, metal detector
W: Jack8, bigler
MK: Jack2, bigler
N: metal detector's signal

SCENE 46
CH: Gwen
L: Photo booth, EXT,DAY
PD:
P:
W: Gwen 10

MK: Gwen 2
N:

SCENE 47
CH: Gwen , Mika
L: Phone Booth, EXT/INT, DAY
PD: fish table
P: Guttering knife, fish
W: Gwen10, Mika
MK: Gwen
N: Sam's over the phone lines

SCENE 47A
CH: Sam
L; Dr. Sam office, INT, DAY
PD: Dr. Sam's office set dress
P: Magazine w/ Sam's picture "New visionary bring Gift of sight"
W: Dr. Sam
MK: Dr. Sam
N: Sam picks up Gwen's call

SCENE 48
CH: Sam
L: Dr. Sam office, INT, DAY
PD: Dr. Sam's office set dress
P: Magazine w/ Sam's picture "New visionary bring Gift of sight"
W: Dr. Sam
MK: Dr. Sam
N: on the phone w/ Gwen

SCENE 48A
CH: Gwen
L: Phone booth, INT, DAY
PD:
P:
W: Gwen10
MK: Gwen 2
N: insert of shoot of Jack's speedboat passes by, on the phone w/ Sam

SCENE 49

CH: Sam

L: Dr. Sam's office, INT, DAY

PD: Dr. Sam office, INT, DAY

P: Magazine w/ Sam's picture "New visionary bring Gift of sight"

W: Dr. Sam

MK: Dr. Sam

N:

SCENE 50

CH: Gwen, Mika

L: Phone Booth, INT/EXT, DAY

PD: Fish table, phone booth

P: Fish gutter knife(cleaver), big fish

W: Gwen10

MK: Gwen 2

N: Chopped fish head off (insert)

SCENE 51

CH: Jack, Kari, Ed

L: Ed's yacht, INT/EXT, DAY

PD: Yacht

P: Jack's sunglasses, fish, Kari's necklace

W: Jack8, Kari's sexy dress, Ed

MK: Jack2, kari, Ed

N: close set, inside yacht

SCENE 52

CH: Jack, Gwen

L: BG living room, kitchen area , INT, DAY

PD: BG living room, kitchen area

P: Bottle of booze, glasses, trash can, jack's fish, Jack's sunglasses, Jack's contacts

W: Jack8, Gwen10

MK: Jack2, Gwen2

N: Need stunt coordinate

SCENE 53

CH: Jack, Gretchen, Kari, Ed, Extras
L: Light House Restaurant, INT, NIGHT
PD: Restaurant/Bar area
P: Jack's contacts, Kari's necklace, glasses, drinks
W: Jack8, Kari, Ed, Gretchen
MK: Jack2, Kari, Ed, Gretchen
N: Background boats, extras

SCENE 54
CH: Gwen
L: Phone Booth, INT, NIGHT
PD:
P:
W: Gwen10
MK: Gwen 2
N:

SCENE 55
CH: Gwen
L: Phone Booth, INT, NIGHT
PD:
P:
W: Gwen10
MK: Gwen 2
N: Sobbing Gwen talks to Sam

SCENE 55A
CH: Sam
L: Dr. Sam's office, INT, NIGHT
PD: Dr. Sam's office
P: Paper piles on desk, Horton's picture
W: Sam
MK: Sam
N: Gwen line over the phone

SCENE 56
CH: Jack, Kari
L: Ed's Yacht, EXT, NIGHT

PD:

P: Wine bottle, wine glasses, kari's necklace, Jack's contacts

W: Kari (from scn 53?), Jack8

MK: Kari, Jack2

N: Stunt, Kari's double, provide warmth for Kari's double

SCENE 57

CH: Gwen, Jack

L: BG Living room

PD: BG Living room

P: Drinks, fake blood, Jack's contacts

W: Gwen10, Jack8

MK: Gwen2, Jack 2

N: Gwen's cloths gets ripped and tear(need double), nose bleed, Stunt Co, close set

SCENE 58

CH: Jack, Gwen

L: BG Pool area, EXT, NIGHT

PD: BG Pool area

P: Jack's contacts, fake blood, Kari's necklace

W: Gwen10(ripped cloth), Jack8

MK: Jack2, Gwen2

N: Jack drops in water, provide warmth

SCENE 59

CH: Jack, Gwen

L: BG Bathroom (shower)/Bedroom

PD: BG Bathroom, wall decal, bedroom

P:

W: Towel wrapped Gwen, Jack PJs

MK: Gwen2 after shower

N: Gwen's naked in shower, closed set

SCENE 60

CH: Jack, Horton, Gwen

L: Wood wall area, EXT, NIGHT

PD: Foggy
P: Jack's contacts, Horton's contacts, fake blood
W: Jack, Horton, Gwen(bloody)
MK: Jack2, Horton
FX MK: Gwen dead, Horton with no eyes.
N: Stunt, long time for fx makeup

SCENE 61
CH: Sam, Earl, Dell
L: Old Dock, EXT, DAY
PD: Shuttle boat
P: Sam's cell, small bag
W: Sam1
MK: Sam
N:

SCENE 62
CH: Sam
L: BG Entrance, DAY, EXT/INT
PD:
P: Sam's bag
W: sam1
MK: Sam
N:

SCENE 63
CH: Jack, Sam
L: BG Bar area, INT, DAY
PD: Record player
P: Limes, large knife, jack's drink
W: Sam1, Jack9
MK: Sam, Jack2
N: Stunt, Knife safety

SCENE 64
CH: Sam
L: BG Bedroom, INT,DAY

PD: BG Bedroom w/ lamp
P: Lamp
W: Sam1
MK: Sam
N:

SCENE 65
CH: Jack
L: BG Hallway, INT, DAY
PD:
P:
W: Jack 9
MK: Jack 2
N:

SCENE 66
CH: Jack, Sam
L: BG Bedroom/Hallway, INT, DAY
PD: BG Bedroom
P: Lamp
W: Sam1, Jack9
MK: Sam(Sweating), Jack2
N: Swing Lamp(lamp double) , Stunt

SCENE 67
CH: Gwen, Gretchen, Sheriff, Deputy, Clarence, Ed, Mamie, Kari's double, Bobby Extras
L: Old Dock, EXT, DAY
PD:
P: Sheriff, Deputy's props, Radios, cover for Kari's body
W: Gwen11, Gretchen1, Sheriff Uniform, Deputy Uniform, everyone else as SCN68
MK: Gwen 2, Gretchen, Kari's body
N: dangerous location can't have too many people on there, Kari's double in water(provide warmth), extras

SCENE 68
CH: Gwen, Gretchen, Sheriff, Deputy, Clarence, Ed, Mamie, Kari's double, Bobby

Extras
L: Trail, EXT, DAY
PD: Dug hole
P: Human bone hand, diamond ring, metal detector, Sheriff's props
W: Gwen11, Gretchen1, Sheriff Uniform, Deputy Uniform, everyone else same as SN67
MK:Gwen2
N: windy set, extras, double check on Wardrobe, makeup continuity

SCENE 69
CH: Gwen, Gretchen
L: Gretchen's boathouse, EXT, DAY
PD:
P:
W: Gwen 11, Gretchen1
MK: Gwen2, Gretchen
N: start inside if rain

SCENE 70
CH: Gwen, Gretchen
L: Gretchen's Boathouse, INT, DAY
PD: Messy, newspapers
P: Serial killer news clippings, Horton's framed pictures(2b/w, 1 colored), Young Gretchen's pictures, Victim #1's pictures
W: Gwen 11, Gretchen1
MK: Gwen2, Gretchen
N:

SCENE 71
CH: Gwen
L: BG Entrance, EXT/INT, NIGHT
PD:
P:
W: Gwen11
MK: Gwen2
N:

SCENE 72

CH: Gwen
L: BG Entrance, INT, NIGHT
PD:
P: Sam's small bag
W: Gwen 11
MK: Gwen 2
N: Gwen react to the opera playing

SCENE 73
CH: Jack, Gwen, Sam(dead)
L: BG Bar area, INT, NIGHT
PD: BG Bar area,
P: Drink, Eyes Martini
W: Jack 9, Gwen 11, Sam1,
MK: Jack 3, Gwen 2-3
FX MK: Sam's eyes bloody hole
N: Loud opera music, long time for fx makeup

SCENE 74
CH: Gwen
L: BG Entrance, EXT, NIGHT
PD:
P:
W: Gwen 11
MK: Gwen 2-3
N: Gwen runs out from bungalow after she saw Sam's body

SCENE 74A
CH: Earl, Dell, Gwen
L: Phone booth Dock, EXT, NIGHT
PD: Fishing supplies, Phone booth, Earl, Dell's Boat
P: Fish gutting knife, cut phone wire
W: Gwen 11
MK: Gwen 3
N: Earl, Dell on a boat(can we see them) at night?

SCENE 75
CH: Gwen

L: Gretchen's Boathouse, EXT, NIGHT
PD:
P: Gwen's fish knife
W: Gwen 11
MK: Gwen 3
N: Real knife on set

SCENE 76
CH: Gwen, Jack
L: Gretchen's boathouse, INT, NIGHT
PD: Serial killer news clippings arranged in order, Horton's shrine
P: Gwen's knife, Jack's Knife
W: Gwen 11, Jack 9
MK: Gwen3, Jack3
N: Knife, Stunt

SCENE 77
CH: Jack, Gwen, Gretchen(dead)
L: Gretchen's boathouse deep inside , INT, NIGHT
PD: More things everywhere
P: Gwen's Knife, Jack's Knife, Gretchen's nose, Gretchen hang in closet
W: Gwen 11, Jack 9
MK: Gwen3, Jack3
FXMK: Gretchen's nose cutoff
N: Knife, Stunt, long time for fx makeup

SCENE 78
CH: Jack, Gwen
L: Gretchen's boathouse, hiding spot, INT/EXT, NIGHT
PD: Footprints
P: Gwen's knife, Jack's Knife, fake mudd
W: Gwen 11(muddy), Jack 9
MK: Gwen3, Jack3
N: Knife

SCENE 79
CH: Gwen
L: Gretchen's boathouse hiding spot, EXT,NIGTH

PD:
P: Gwen's Knife, fake mudd
W: Gwen 11(muddy)
MK: Gwen 3
N: Hiding area safety(bugs,rust), Knife

SCENE 80
CH: Jack, Gwen, Sheriff Whitman
L: Old dock, EXT, NIGHT
PD:
P: Gwen's knife, Jack, Knife, Sheriff's props, fake blood
W: Gwen 11(muddy), Jack 9, Sheriff's uniform
MK: Gwen3, Jack3, Sheriff
FXMK: Sheriff throat clutched, Jack stabbed through item
N: Stunt, dangerous location, limited crew

SCENE 81
CH: Gwen, Jack's body, Sheriff' body (double)
L: Old dock, EXT,NIGHT
PD:
P: Gwen's knife, Jack's knife
W: Gwen 11(muddy), Jack 9, Sheriff's uniform
MK: Gwen3
N: dangerous location, limited crew

SCENE 82:
CH: Gwen, Jack's body, Sheriff' body (double), deputy #1, #2
L: Old dock, EXT,NIGHT
PD:
P: Blanket
W: Gwen 11(muddy), Deputy #1, #2's uniforms
MK: Gwen3-4
N: dangerous location, limited crew

SCENE 83
CH: Gwen Pregnant, Students
L: Gwen's classroom, INT, DAY

""In The Eyes Of The Beholder"" Report created Sun, Feb 18, 2007 Page 1

April Day of Month:	10	11	12	13	14	15	16	17	18	19	20	21	22	23	24	25	26	27	Co.	
Day Of Week:	Tue	Wed	Thu	Fri	Sat	Sun	Mon	Tue	Wed	Thu	Fri	Sat	Sun	Mon	Tue	Wed	Thu	Fri	Travel	Travel
Shooting Days:	1	2	3	4	5		6	7	8	9	10	11		12	13	14	15	16		
AERIALS									SWF											
STEADI-POD									SWF											
UNDERWATER CAMERA									SWF											

""In The Eyes Of The Beholder"" Report created Sun, Feb 18, 2007 Page 2

Day of Month: Day Of Week: Shooting Days:	Work	Hold	Holiday	Start	Finish	TOTAL
BLACKBOARD	2			4/13	4/14	2
CLOCK ON NIGHTSTAND	1			4/26	4/26	1
COFFEE TABLE	1			4/16	4/16	1
DECK CHAIRS	1			4/21	4/21	1
DESK/CHAIR	3			4/10	4/14	3
END TABLES	1			4/16	4/16	1
FILING CABINET	1			4/10	4/10	1
FISH GUTTING STATION	1			4/23	4/23	1
GARLAND	1			4/16	4/16	1
LEATHER STRAPS	1			4/12	4/12	1
MEDICAL TABLE/GERNEY	1			4/12	4/12	1
OVER-FLOWING ASHTRA	1			4/16	4/16	1
PIANO						
POOL TABLE	1			4/26	4/26	1
RESTAURANT PATIO TAB	1			4/19	4/19	1
SIDE CHAIRS	1			4/10	4/10	1
SMALL LIGHT	1			4/25	4/25	1
SMALL NIGHT LAMP	1			4/26	4/26	1
STACKS OF OLD NEWSPA	1			4/16	4/16	1
WAITING ROOM CHAIRS	2			4/10	4/11	2

""In The Eyes Of The Beholder"" Report created Sun, Feb 18, 2007 Page 1

April Day of Month:	10	11	12	13	14	15	16	17	18	19	20	21	22	23	24	25	26	27	Co.	
Day Of Week:	Tue	Wed	Thu	Fri	Sat	Sun	Mon	Tue	Wed	Thu	Fri	Sat	Sun	Mon	Tue	Wed	Thu	Fri	Travel	Travel
Shooting Days:	1	2	3	4	5		6	7	8	9	10	11		12	13	14	15	16		
BELL RINGS				SWF																
CREAK															SWF					
CRICKETS																SWF				
DOOR CREAK																SWF				
JACK & GWEN FIGHTING																	SWF			
LAUGHTER										SWF										
MOANING SOUNDS								SWF												
MOS		SW					W	W							WF					
ROAR OF CHEERS					SWF															
RUSTLE															SWF					
SOFT MUSIC								SWF												
THUD									SW							WF				
TICKING CLOCK																SWF				
UPBEAT MUSIC										SWF										

""In The Eyes Of The Beholder"" Report created Sun, Feb 18, 2007 Page 2

Day of Month: Day Of Week: Shooting Days:	Work	Hold	Holiday	Start	Finish	TOTAL
BESSIE-MESSED UP HAIR	1			4/16	4/16	1
BLOOD	4			4/11	4/26	4
BROWN CONTACTS	5			4/10	4/17	5
DR R'S EYES CUTOUT	1			4/25	4/25	1
GWEN-GREY STREAK IN I	2			4/12	4/14	2
GWEN-SPECIAL HAIR DO	1			4/16	4/16	1
ICEY BLUE CONTACTS	13			4/11	4/26	13
JACK-DEAD-PURPLE, BLC	1			4/18	4/18	1
JULIE-DEAD-PURPLE, BL(	2			4/20	4/23	2
SWEAT	3			4/19	4/26	3
TATOOS	1			4/12	4/12	1
WEDDING MAKEUP	1			4/16	4/16	1

""In The Eyes Of The Beholder"" Report created Sun, Feb 18, 2007 Page 1

April Day of Month:	10	11	12	13	14	15	16	17	18	19	20	21	22	23	24	25	26	27	Co.	
Day Of Week:	Tue	Wed	Thu	Fri	Sat	Sun	Mon	Tue	Wed	Thu	Fri	Sat	Sun	Mon	Tue	Wed	Thu	Fri	Travel	Travel
Shooting Days:	1	2	3	4	5		6	7	8	9	10	11		12	13	14	15	16		
BOWLING SHIRTS					SWF															
CATHERINE-DAY 13 WAR								SWF												
CATHERINE-DAY 16 WAR			SWF																	
CATHERINE-DAY 3 WARE					SWF															
CATHERINE-DAY 5 WARE		SWF																		
CATHERINE-DAY 6 WARE		SWF																		
CATHERINE-DAY 8 WARE							SWF													
CATHERINE-WEDDING O							SWF													
CLARENCE-HAT											SW					WF				
CREAM WEDDING DRESS							SWF													
DELL-DAY 13 WARDROB														SWF						
DELL-DAY 14 WARDROB									SW		W			WF						
DEPUTY UNIFORM(S)								SW	W					W		WF				
DOCMASTER-DAY 13 WA														SWF						
DOCTOR'S SUIT			SWF																	
DR. LAB COATS	SWF																			
DR. R-DAY 14 WARDROB	SW																			
DR. R-SUIT & LAB COAT	SW	WF														W	WF			
EARL-DAY 13 WARDROB														SWF						
EARL-DAY 14 WARDROB									SW		W			WF						
GROOM TUXEDO							SWF													
GWEN-BATHING SUIT															SWF					
GWEN-DAY 10 WARDROB					SWF															
GWEN-DAY 11 WARDROB										SW	W					WF				
GWEN-DAY 12 WARDROB															SWF					
GWEN-DAY 13 WARDROB															SW		W	WF		
GWEN-DAY 14 WARDROB	SW						W		W	W	W			W	W	W	W	WF		
GWEN-DAY 16 WARDROB					SWF															
GWEN-DAY 2 WARDROBE	SW			WF																
GWEN-DAY 3 WARDROBE					SWF															
GWEN-DAY 5 WARDROBE		SWF																		
GWEN-DAY 6 WARDROBE		SWF																		
GWEN-DAY 7 WARDROBE							SWF													
GWEN-DAY 8 WARDROBE							SWF													
GWEN-DAY 9 WARDROBE								SWF												
GWEN-DINNER DRESS								SW		W					W	W	WF			
GWEN-DINNER JACKET										SW						W	WF			
GWEN-JACKET																				
GWEN-JACKET W/POCKE	SW			W			W		W	W	W			W	W	W	W	WF		
GWEN-NIGHTGOWN								SW							W		WF			
HOSPITAL GOWN		SWF																		
JACK-BELT															SWF					
JACK-DARK SUIT	SW			WF																
JACK-DAY 10 WARDROBE					SWF															
JACK-DAY 11 WARDROBE										SW	W					WF				
JACK-DAY 12 WARDROBE										SW					W	W	WF			
JACK-DAY 13 WARDROBE										SW	W	W		W	W		WF			

""In The Eyes Of The Beholder"" Report created Sun, Feb 18, 2007 Page 1

April Day of Month:	10	11	12	13	14	15	16	17	18	19	20	21	22	23	24	25	26	27	Co.	
Day Of Week:	Tue	Wed	Thu	Fri	Sat	Sun	Mon	Tue	Wed	Thu	Fri	Sat	Sun	Mon	Tue	Wed	Thu	Fri	Travel	Travel
Shooting Days:	1	2	3	4	5		6	7	8	9	10	11		12	13	14	15	16		
1. JACK	SW	W	H	W	W		W	W	W	W	W	W		W	W	W	WF			
2. GWEN	SW	W	W	W	W		W	W	W	W	W	H		W	W	W	W	WF		
3. DR. RIELAND	SW	WD														PW	WF			
4. CATHERINE		SW	W	H	W		W	WF												
5. JULIE										SW	W	W		WF						
6. MARLIN										SW	W	H		WF						
7. TERRENCE			SWF																	
8. CLARENCE										SW	W	H		H	H	WF				
9. DELL									SW	H	W	H		WF						
10. EARL									SW	H	W	H		WF						
11. SHERIFF									SW	H	H	H		W	H	WF				
12. DEPUTY								SW	W	H	H	H		W	H	WF				
13. MAMIE										SWF										
14. STUDENT				SW	WF															
15. BESSIE							SWF													
16. BARTENDER										SWF										
17. NURSE	SW	WF																		
18. DOCK MASTER														SWF						
19. CREW #1											SWF									
20. DOCTOR #1	SW	W	WF																	
21. DOCTOR #2		SWF																		
22. DOCTOR #3			SWF																	
23. WARDEN			SWF																	
24. GUARD #1			SWF																	
25. GUARD #2			SWF																	
26. OLD MAN #1																		SWF		
27. OPERATOR V/O																		SWF		
28. MARTY					SWF															
29. BRIAN				SW	WF															
30. MEDICAL ASST.		SWF																		
31. YOUNG GIRL							SWF													
32. INSULIN GIRL										SWF										
33. OLD MAN #2											SW	H		WF						
34. CORONER									SW	H	H	H		W	H	WF				

""In The Eyes Of The Beholder"" Report created Sun, Feb 18, 2007 Page 1

April Day of Month:	10	11	12	13	14	15	16	17	18	19	20	21	22	23	24	25	26	27	Co. Travel	Travel
Day Of Week:	Tue	Wed	Thu	Fri	Sat	Sun	Mon	Tue	Wed	Thu	Fri	Sat	Sun	Mon	Tue	Wed	Thu	Fri		
Shooting Days:	1	2	3	4	5		6	7	8	9	10	11		12	13	14	15	16		
BERKHIEMER HOUSEBOA											SW	W		WF						
DUCK SOUP									SW		W			W	WF					
FERRY											SWF									
GWEN'S RENTAL CAR							SWF													
LIMO							SWF													
PATROL BOAT(S)									SWF											
PLATFORM BOAT											SW			WF						
ROW BOAT									SW		W			WF						

""In The Eyes Of The Beholder"" Report created Sun, Feb 18, 2007 Page 2

Day of Month: Day Of Week: Shooting Days:	Work	Hold	Holiday	Start	Finish	TOTAL
AERIALS	1			4/18	4/18	1
STEADI-POD	1			4/18	4/18	1
UNDERWATER CAMERA	1			4/18	4/18	1

""In The Eyes Of The Beholder"" Report created Sun, Feb 18, 2007 Page 4

Day of Month: Day Of Week: Shooting Days:	Work	Hold	Holiday	Start	Finish	TOTAL
JACK-DAY 14 WARDROBE	2			4/18	4/25	2
JACK-DAY 2 WARDROBE						
JACK-DAY 3 WARDROBE	1			4/14	4/14	1
JACK-DAY 7 WARDROBE	1			4/16	4/16	1
JACK-DAY 8 WARDROBE	1			4/16	4/16	1
JACK-DAY 9 WARDROBE	1			4/17	4/17	1
JACK-DINNER JACKET	1			4/19	4/19	1
JACK-JACKET W/POCKET	4			4/19	4/26	4
JACK-PAJAMAS W/POCKE	4			4/17	4/26	4
JULIE-BLOUSE	4			4/19	4/23	4
JULIE-DAY 11 WARDROBI	1			4/20	4/20	1
JULIE-DAY 13 WARDROBI	4			4/19	4/23	4
JULIE-REVEALING BIKINI	1			4/23	4/23	1
MARLIN-DAY 11 WARDRO	1			4/20	4/20	1
MARLIN-DAY 13 WARDRO	3			4/19	4/23	3
NURSE UNIFORM	1			4/10	4/10	1
OLD BATHROBE W/STAIN	1			4/16	4/16	1
PRISON GUARD UNIFORM	1			4/12	4/12	1
PRISON INMATE SUIT	1			4/12	4/12	1
PRISON WARDEN SUIT	1			4/12	4/12	1
RESORT UNIFORMS	4			4/19	4/25	4
SHERIFF UNIFORM	3			4/18	4/25	3
SHERIFF-COWBOY HAT	3			4/18	4/25	3
SURGERY SCRUBS	2			4/10	4/11	2
SURGICAL MASK	1			4/11	4/11	1
WEDDING VEIL	1			4/16	4/16	1

In Eyes of the Beholder

10th Revised Schedule

(Ken Blevins
Roddi Crowley)

Day	Date	Wkday	Set	Scenes	Crew Call	Crew Wrap	1st Meal	2nd Meal
1	12-Nov	Mon	BG Ent/Living room EXT, BG Poolside EXT, Speedboat EXT, BG Living Rm INT, BG Ent EXT/INT	(B25)26,38,42,52,72,30	8AM	8PM	7.30AM	2PM
2	13-Nov	Tue Sam	BG Ent EXT/INT, BG Living Rm INT, BG Hallway, BG Bedroom	62,63,64,65,66,73	8AM	8PM	7.30AM	2PM
3	14-Nov	Wed Sam	Arriving Dock EXT, Store INT, Woodwall EXT, Treelined area EXT	41,(*42), 43,44,61,40,19,60,6	9AM	9PM	8.30AM	3PM
4	15-Nov	Thu	Trail EXT, Picnic EXT Company move Donald's boat	45,35,36,39, (51), 56	9AM	9PM	8.30AM	3PM
5	16-Nov	Fri	BG LivingRmTableINT, BG livingRm,Patio,Pool INT/EXT	34,57,58	10AM	10PM	9.30AM	4PM
6	17-Nov	Sat	BG Bathroom INT Bedroom INT, Jack's Bedroom INT	28,32,*59, COMPANY MOVE 59a, 31,32,33,11 (D for N, all scenes)	11AM	11PM	10.30AM	5PM
	18-Nov	Sun	DAY OFF					
	19-Nov	Mon	DAY OFF					
7	20-Nov	Tue Sheriff Gretchen	Trail EXT, Company move ArrivingDock EXT, Restaurant INT/EXT Viewing Room INT	68,37,24*.2*	9AM	9PM	8.30AM	3PM
8	21-Nov	Wed Sheriff Gretchen	Arriving Dock EXT, Old Dock EXT	67,80,81,82	12PM	12AM	11.30 AM	6PM
	22-Nov 23-Nov	Thu Fri	Thanksgiving 2 Days OFF					
9	24-Nov	Sat	U Campus EXT, U Lecture Hall INT	84,4,83,22,3, (21)-B	8AM	8PM	7.30AM	2PM
10	25-Nov	Sun	Sally's House EXT, PhoneBooth EXT, Arriving Dock EXT	5, COMPANY MOVE 46,47*, 48*,50,54, 55*, 74*, COMPANY MOVE, 74a	9AM	9PM	8.30AM	3PM
11	26-Nov	Mon Gretchen	Arriving Dock EXT, Company move Restaurant INT/EXT	23,24A*, 27,29, 53	10AM	10PM	9.30AM	4PM
12 WRAP DELTA	27-Nov	Tues Gretchen	Gretchen's Home INT/EXT	69,70,75,76,77,78,79	11AM	11PM	10.30 AM	5PM
	28-Nov	Wed	DAY OFF					
	29-Nov	Thurs	DAY OFF					
13	30 -Nov	Fri	Jack's House EXT/INT	84,20,7,8,9, 10,14	12PM	12AM	11.30PM	6PM
14	1-Dec	Sat	DR Sam'sOffice INT, Prison HallwayINT, Execution Rm/Press Rm INT	12,47A, 48A, 49, 55A,1,2A	11AM	11PM	10.30PM	5PM
15	2-Dec	Sun	Hospital Rm INT, Hospital Ent EXT, OR INT	16,17,18, 13,15	11AM	11PM	10.30AM	5PM

Can we shoot the OR scenes Early & the conference.

DAY 9, Nov. 24th - CALL TIME @ 8AM in Elk Grove

Isleton Police Dept 100 2nd St, Isleton, CA (4.88 miles away) 916-777-7774	Isleton Fire Dept 201 2nd St, Isleton, CA (4.87 miles away) 916-777-7776	Antioch Convalescent Hospital 1210 A St, Antioch, CA (14.96 miles away) 925-757-8787

CALL SHEET

"In the Eyes of the Beholder"

PRODUCTION OFFICE:
ADDRESS
TELEPHONE NUMBER: (916) 370 5615

Director: *Louis Mandylor*
Producer: *Mamie Jean Colvert*
1st A.D.: *Serenity Pang-Bellman*

DAY 1

LOCATION:151 Brannan Island Rd Isleton, CA 95641-9767 PHONE: (916) 777 5901

Nov-12, 1/15

CREW CALL ON LOCATION: 8AM

EST WRAP: 8PM

Weather: Partly cloudy Temp: 40F-66F
Sunrise: 6:41AM Sunset: 5PM

Sc No.	PG	Set	Synopsis	Character	Artist	P/U	M/U	W/D
26	2/8	bungalow entrance/ living room,INT	*Jack and Gwen first see bungalow and kiss*	*Jack Gwen*		*TIME*	*TIME*	
38	1	bungalow poolside,EXT	*Jack wakes up with hangover, fights w/ Gwen, leaves*	*Jack Gwen*	*NAME*	*MOW*	*TIME*	
42	1/8	bungalow poolside, speedboat,EXT	Jack on speedboat,Gwen storms back into bungalow	Jack Gwen				
25	1/8	bungalow, EXT	Bungalow establish shoot			MOW	TIME	
			2nd Meal: 2PM					
52	2	bungalow living rm,INT	*Jack returns from fishing, fight w/ Gwen, storms off*	*Jack Gwen*	*NAME*			
30	3/8	bungalow docks, EXT	*Jack is drunk, singing, walking back to bungalow w/ Gwen*	*Jack Gwen*	*NAME*			
71	1/8	bungalow entrance, EXT	Gwen returns from Gretchen's	Gwen	*NAME*	MOW	TIME	
72	1/8	bungalow entrance, INT	Gwen returns from Gretchen's, notices Sam's bag	Gwen				

ADDITIONAL EQUIPMENT

Speedboat Scn 42
Dolly, Tracks

PROPS/Pro Design

Production Design *Record Player*

Props	LDs,Newspaper, coffee, Jack'sunglasses,Bottle of booze, glasses, trash can, jack's fish, Jack's contacts	jack's fish, Gwen's sunglasse s	Jack's contacts, trash can,Sam's small bag

Wardrobe

Jack, Gwen

MAKE UP

Jack, Gwen

Special FX Make up

CAST NAME

LOCATION NOTES / PARKING

Parking is available in the resort.

SPECIAL NOTES

Enclosed shoes must be worn at all times on set.
Scn 52 Need stunt coordination

Producer: Mamie Jean Calvert		PA	Arnold Carter
Exe Producer	Robert Calvert	PA	Rod Retamoza
Exe Producer	Jacqueline C. Reiland	PA	David Ferrero
Exe Producer	Witt Widmer	PA	Jeff Smith
Exe Producer	Judy Nessun	PA	
Exe Producer	Carolyn and Jo	PA	
Assistant Producer	Linda Arslanian		
Co-Producer	Joel Fox		
Director	Louis Mandylor		
Director of Photography	Ted		
Assistant Director	Serenity Pang-Bellman		
UPM	Charlene Agabao		
Script Supervisor	Judy Nessun		
Gaffer	Nghia Khuu		
1st Assistant Camera			
Best Boy	Samuel Kim		
Key Grip			
Prouction Designer	Janene White		
Prop Master			
Wardrobe			
Key make-up Artist	Barbara Mcgee		
SPFX make up Artist	Heather Foote		
Sound Mixer	Joe Stillwater		
Boom Operator			
Stunt Coordinator	John Ayers		
Electrician	Ben Casias		
Electrician			
Electrician			
Grip			
Grip			
Grip			
Key PA	Tony Randolph		

Isleton Police Dept 100 2nd St, Isleton, CA (4.88 miles away) 916-777-7774	Isleton Fire Dept 201 2nd St, Isleton, CA (4.87 miles away) 916-777-7776	Antioch Convalescent Hospital 1210 A St, Antioch, CA (14.96 miles away)

CALL SHEET

"In the Eyes of the Beholder"

PRODUCTION OFFICE:
ADDRESS
TELEPHONE NUMBER: (916) 370 5615

Director *Louis Mandylor*
Producer *Mamie Jean Calvert*
1st A.D. *Serenity Pang-Bellman*

DAY 3

LOCATION: 15476 Highway 160 Isleton, CA 95641-9767 PHONE: (916) 777 5901

Nov-14, 11/14

CREW CALL ON LOCATION: 9AM

EST WRAP: 9PM

Weather: Mostly Sunny Temp: 50F-71F

Wind Avg: 7 mph, 10 am - 4pm

High Tide: 7:54am/5:21pm-Low Tide:1:0

Sunrise: 6:46AM Sunset: 4:55PM

Sc No	PG	Set	Synopsis	Character	Artist	P/U	M/U	W/D
41		Speedboat	Jack goes cruising on boat	Jack		*TIME*	*TIME*	
*42		Speedboat	Jack heads to trail	Jack	*NAME*	*MOW*	*TIME*	
43		Speedboat	Gwen POV - Jack speeds by	Jack				
44		Shore	Jack ties up boat	Jack				
61	Ext: Arriving drrives, sees Dell and, Dell, Earl							
			COMPANY MOVE - EDIE MART					
			2nd Meal: 3PM					
40	Int. Edie Mar:k rents boat from GrJack, Grady							
			COMPANY MOVE- RESORT - FORREST					
19		Ext: Resort Forrest-woodpile	Dream: Horton/Jack POV killing Gwen	Jack, Gwen	*NAME*			
60		Ext: Resort Forrest-open field	Horton/Jack kills Gwen, has no eyes, reveal:Jack as Horton	Jack, Gwen	*NAME*			
6		Ext: Resort Forrest - tree area	B-movie: Frightened Woman is chased by Psychopath, gets trapped, screams	Frightened Woman, Psychopath		MOW	TIME	

ADDITIONAL EQUIPMENT

PROPS/Pro Design

Production Design	
PROPS	Jack's sunglasses, Sam's bag, Psycho knife, Jack's contacts, key for boat, cash

Wardrobe

Jack, Sam, Dell, Ea

MAKE UP

Jack, Sam, Dell, Ea

Special FX Make up

Jack - eyeless

LOCATION NOTES / PARKING

Dress warm for Night, water, and forrest

SPECIAL NOTES

Special FX make-up for Jack

Producer	Mamie Jean Calvert	PA	Arnold Carter
Exe Producer	Robert Calvert	PA	Rod Retamoza
Exe Producer	Jacqueline C. Reil	PA	David Ferrero
Exe Producer	Witt Widmer	PA	Jeff Smith
Exe Producer	Judy Nessun	PA	
Exe Producer	Carolyn and Jo	PA	
Assistant Producer	Linda Arslanian		
Co-Producer	Joel Fox		
Director	Louis Mandylor		
Director of Photog:	Ted		
Assistant Director	Serenity Pang-Bellman		
UPM	Charlene Agabao		
Script Supervisor	Judy Nessun		
Gaffer	Nghia Khuu		
1st Assistant Camera			
Best Boy	Samuel Kim		
Key Grip			
Prouction Designer	Janene White		
Prop Master			
Wardrobe			
Key make-up Artist	Barbara Mcgee		
SPFX make up Artist	Heather Foote		
Sound Mixer	Joe Stillwater		
Boom Operator			
Stunt Coordinator	John Ayers		
Electrician	Ben Casias		
Electrician			

Isleton Police Dept 100 2nd St, Isleton, CA (4.88 miles away) 916-777-7774	Isleton Fire Dept 201 2nd St, Isleton, CA (4.87 miles away) 916-777-7776	Antioch Convalescent Hospital 1210 A St, Antioch, CA (14.96 miles away) 925-757-8787

CAI

"In the Eyes of the Beholder"

PRODUCTION OFFICE:
ADDRESS
TELEPHONE NUMBER: (916) 370 5615

Director: *Louis Mandylor*
Producer: *Mamie Jean Calve*
1st A.D.: *Serenity Pang-Be*

DAY 4

LOCATION: 15476 Highway 160 Isleton, CA 95641-9767 PHONE: (916) 777 5901

11/15/0'

CREW CALL ON LOCATION: 9AM

Weather: Mostly Sunny Temp: 48F-69F

Sc No.	PG	Set	Synopsis	Character	Artist	P/U
45		EXT: North Trail	Jack meets Bigler, scares him away	Jack, Bigler		*TIME*
35		EXT: North Trail	Jack and Gwen frolic	Jack, Gwen	*NAME*	*MOW*
36		EXT: North Trail	Jack and Gwen picnic and talk	Jack, Gwem		
			COMPANY MOVE - ARRIVING DOCK			
			2nd Meal: 3PM			
39		EXT: Donalds' yacht	Kari flirts w/Jack, gets caught by Donalds	Jack, Donalds, Kari	*NAME*	
51		EXT/INT: Donalds' yacht	Kari dances for Donalds, Jack watches	Jack, Donalds, Kari	*NAME*	
56		EXT: Donalds' yacht	Jack talks to Kari, kills her	Jack, Kari		MOW

3rd Meal : 9PM

ADDITIONAL EQUIPMENT

PROPS/Pro Design

Production Design

PROPS	Jack's sunglasses, picnic blanket, picnic basket/bag, Bigler's metal detector, Gwen's sunglasses, glasses of wine

Wardrobe

Jack, Gwen, Bigler, D

MAKE UP

Jack, Gwen Bigler, Do

Special FX Make up

LOCATION NOTES / PARKING

NEED PA WATCHING ROAD OUTSIDE OF ARRIVING DOCK, W/VEST AND CONES
Minimum grips/electricians today

SPECIAL NOTES

IF KARI OR STUNTMAN IN WIG FALLS IN WATER, NEED BLANKET, TOWELS, ETC
NEED STANDBY LIFESAVER, LIFEJACKET FOR WATER STUNT

Producer:	Mamie Jean Calvert	PA	Arnold Carter
Exe Producer	Robert Calvert	PA	Rod Retamoza
Exe Producer	Jacqueline C. Reilanc	PA	David Ferrero
Exe Producer	Witt Widmer	PA	Jeff Smith
Exe Producer	Judy Nessen	PA	
Exe Producer	Carolyn Munson		
Exe Producer	Jo Hoffmeier	PA	
Assistant Producer	Linda Arslanian		
Co-Producer	Zach Thomson		
Co-Producer	Joel Fox		
Director	Louis Mandylor		
Director of Photograp	Ted Caloroso		
Assistant Director	Serenity Pang-Bellman		
UPM	Charlene Agabao		
Script Supervisor	Judy Nessen		
Gaffer	Nghia Khuu		
1st Assistant Camera	Amy _______		
Best Boy	Samuel Kim		
Key Grip	Ryan Baustian		
Prouction Designer	Janene White		
Prop Master	John Ayers		
Wardrobe	Deborah		
Key make-up Artist	Barbara Mcgee		
SPFX make up Artist	Heather Foote		
Sound Mixer	Niko Zasimezuk		
Boom Operator	Jon Vennarucci		
Stunt Coordinator	John Ayers		
Electrician	Ben Casias		
Electrician	Drew _______		
Electrician			
Grip			
Grip			
Grip			

Isleton Police Dept 100 2nd St, Isleton, CA (4.88 miles away) 916-777-7774	Isleton Fire Dept 201 2nd St, Isleton, CA (4.87 miles away) 916-777-7776	Antioch Convalescent Hospital 1210 A St, Antioch, CA (14.96 miles away) 925-757-8787

CALI

"In the Eyes of the Beholder"

PRODUCTION OFFICE:Cabin 1
ADDRESS: Lighthouse Resort
TELEPHONE NUMBER: (916) 370 5615

Director: *Louis Mandylor*
Producer: *Mamie Jean Calve:*
1st A.D.: *Serenity Pang-Be.*

DAY 7

LOCATION: 151 Brannan Island Rd (Lighthouse Resort) Isleton, Ca

11/20/07

CREW CALL ON LOCATION: 9AM

EST WRAP: 9PM

Weather: Mostly Sunny Temp: 40F-65F

Sunrise 6:53AM/ Sunset 4:51PM

Tides: 4 ft./High Tide 12:03AM Low Tide 6:55PM

Sc No.	PG	Set	Synopsis	Character	Artist	P/U
			1st Meal: 8:30AM			
68	1 1/3	EXT: NORTH TRAIL	Sheriff finds body	Gretchen, Gwen, Bigler, Clarence, Deputy		
			COMPANY MOVE – ARRIVING DOCK			
24*	2	EXT: ARRIVING DOCK	Jack POV looking at Sheriff	Jack, Sheriff		
37	3 2/3	INT. RESTAURANT	Jack, Gwen drink w/ Kari, Donalds and Sheriff; Gretchen bartends	Jack, Gwen, Kari, Donalds Sheriff, Gretchen, EXTRAS		
			2nd Meal: 3PM			
*2	>1/3	INT. VIEWING RM	Reverse of Horton's execution	1 Guard, 3 reporters, family members, priest		
			3rd Meal : 9PM			

ADDITIONAL EQUIPMENT

Condor (lift)?

PROPS/Pro Design

PROPS	metal detector, wine glasses, cocktails, food, photos of victims, reported notepads, sunglasses (Jack and Gwen)

Wardrobe

Jack, Gwen, Kari, Donalds, Gretchen, Mamie, Bigler, Clarence, Deputy,

MAKE UP

Jack, Gwen, Kari, Donalds, Gretchen, Mamie, Bigler, Clarence, Deputy, EXTRAS

Special FX Make up

~~[illegible] Dead Kari~~

SPECIAL NOTES

SC. 68, BEWARE OF POISON OAK ON LOCATION

TRAFFIC CONES/FLAH/JACKET FOR TRAIL AND RESTAURANT, DO NOT PARK ON LEVEE!

SC. 24, 37 – HEAVY EXTRAS DAY, BIG YACHT; NEED 34 BOATS FOR SC.37, SAG

SC. 24,37,2- MAKE-UP ASSISTANTS FOR BARBARA, BE SURE TO SHUTTLE TALENT AND

Producer: Mamie Jean Calvert		Key PA	Tony Randolph
Exe Producer	Robert Calvert	PA	Rod Retamoza
Exe Producer	Jacqueline C. Reiland	PA	David Ferrero
Exe Producer	Witt Widmer	PA	Jeff Smith·
Exe Producer	Judy Nessen	PA	Ryan Nelson
Exe Producer	Carolyn Munson		
Exe Producer	Jo Hoffmeier		
Assistant Producer	Linda Arslanian		
Co-Producer	Zach Thomson -		
Co-Producer	Joel Fox		
Director	Louis Mandylor		
Director of Photography	Ted Caloroso		
Assistant Director	Serenity Pang-Bellman		
UPM	Charlene Agabao		
Script Supervisor	Judy Nessen		
Gaffer	Nghia Khuu		
1st Assistant Camera	Amy ______		
Best Boy	Samuel Kim		
Key Grip	Ryan Baustian		
Prouction Designer	Janene White		
Prop Master	John Ayers		
Wardrobe	Deborah		
Key make-up Artist	Barbara Mcgee		
SPFX make up Artist	JD Ayers		
Sound Mixer	Niko Zasimczuk		
Boom Operator	Jon Vennarucci		
Stunt Coordinator	John Ayers		
Electrician	Ben Casias		
Electrician	Drew ______		
Electrician			

Isleton Police Dept	Isleton Fire Dept	Antioch Convalescent Hospital
100 2nd St, Isleton, CA (4.88 miles away) 916-777-7774	201 2nd St, Isleton, CA (4.87 miles away) 916-777-7776	1210 A St, Antioch, CA (14.96 miles away) 925-757-8787

"In the Eyes of the Beholder" CALL SHEET

PRODUCTION OFFICE:Cabin 1
ADDRESS: Lighthouse Resort
TELEPHONE NUMBER: (916) 370 5615

Director: *Louis Mandylor*
Producer: *Mamie Jean Calv*
1st A.D.: *Serenity Pang-B*

DAY 8

LOCATION: 151 Brannan Island Rd (Lighthouse Resort) Isleton, Ca

11/21/07

CREW CALL ON LOCATION: 12PM

EST WRAP: 12PM

Weather: Mostly Sunny Temp: 39F-65F

Sunrise 6:54AM/ Sunset 4:50PM

Tides:4.3 ft./High Tide 12:35AM/Low Tide7:52PM

Sc No.	PG	Set	Synopsis	Character		P/U
			1st Meal: 11:30AM			
67	3	EXT. ARRIVING DOCK	Sheriff finds Kari's dead body	Donalds, Earl, Dell, Bobby, Deputy, Clarence, Gretchen	Gwen, 20+ EXTRAS	
80	4 1/3	EXT: OLD DOCK	Jack chases Gwen, kills Sheriff, Jack dies	Jack, Sheriff, Gwen		
			2nd Meal: 6PM			
81	1/3	EXT: OLD DOCK	Gwen is in shock	Gwen		
82	>1/3	EXT: OLD DOCK	Deputy arrives, puts blanket around Gwen	Deputy, Gwen		

3rd Meal : 12AM

ADDITIONAL EQUIPMENT

Condor (lift)?

PROPS/Pro Design

PROPS	blanket, Kari's necklace, 2 knives,fishing pole, sheet,pole or wood to impale Jack

Wardrobe

Donalds, Earl,Dell, Sheriff +20 EXTRAS	Bobby, Deputy, Clarence, Gretchen,Gwen,Jack

MAKE UP

Donalds, Earl,Dell, +20 EXTRAS	Bobby, Deputy, Clarence, Gretchen,Gwen,Jack

Special FX Make up

67- Dead Kari
80-Sheriff

SPECIAL NOTES

SC. 67, EXTRAS, USE CONES/VERST/FLAGS FOR TRAFFIC CONTROL
TRAFFIC CONES/FLAH/JACKET FOR RESTAURANT, SHUTTLE CREW AND TALENT
SC. 80, STUNT, SPECIAL FX:IMPALING JACK
SC. 24,37,2- MAKE-UP ASSISTANTS FOR BARBARA, BE SURE TO SHUTTLE TALENT ANI

Producer:Mamie Jean Calvert		Key PA	Tony Randolph
Exe Producer	Robert Calvert	PA	Rod Retamoza
Exe Producer	Jacqueline C. Reiland	PA	David Ferrero
Exe Producer	Witt Widmer	PA	Jeff Smith
Exe Producer	Judy Nessen	PA	Ryan Nelson
Exe Producer	Carolyn Munson		
Exe Producer	Jo Hoffmeier		
Assistant Producer	Linda Arslanian		
Co-Producer	Zach Thomson		
Co-Producer	Joel Fox		
Director	Louis Mandylor		
Director of Photography	Ted Caloroso		
Assistant Director	Serenity Pang-Bellman		
UPM	Charlene Agabao		
Script Supervisor	Judy Nessen		
Gaffer	Nghia Khuu		
1st Assistant Camera	Amy ______		
Best Boy	Samuel Kim		
Key Grip	Ryan Baustian		
Prouction Designer	Janene White		
Prop Master	John Ayers		
Wardrobe	Deborah		
Key make-up Artist	Barbara Mcgee		
SPFX make up Artist	JD Ayers		
Sound Mixer	Niko Zasimezuk		
Boom Operator	Jon Vennarucci		
Stunt Coordinator	John Ayers		
Electrician	Ben Casias		
Electrician	Drew ______		
Electrician			
Grip			
Grip			
Grip			

Elk Grove Police 8380 Laguna Palms Way Elk Grove 95758 (916) 478-8000	Elk Grove CSD Fire Dept.(916) 685-9502 8820 Elk Grove Boulevard, Suite 2 Elk Grove, CA 92624	Methodist Hospital 7500 Hospital Dr, Sacramento, CA (916) 423-3000

"In the Eyes of the Beholder" CALL SHEET

PRODUCTION OFFICE: Cabin 1
ADDRESS: Lighthouse Resort
TELEPHONE NUMBER: (916) 370 5615

Director: *Louis Mandylor*
Producer: *Mamie Jean Calve*
1st A.D.: *Serenity Pang-Be.*

DAY 9

LOCATION: University of Phoenix, 9280 W Stockton Blvd, Elk Grove, Ca 95758

11/24/07

CREW CALL ON LOCATION: 8AM

EST WRAP: 8PM

Weather: Mostly Sunny Temp: 40F-65F

Sunrise 6:53AM/ Sunset 4:51PM

Sc No.	PG	Set	Synopsis	Character	Artist	P/U
			1st Meal:7:30AM –	**ON**	**LOCATION**	
21		EXT. UNIVERSITY CAMPUS, DAY	*estb. Shot*	EXTRAS		
		EXT.UNIVERSITY CAMPUS, DAY	Gwen sits w/baby, shakes it	Gwen, Baby, EXTRAS		
84						
4		EXT.UNIVERSITY CAMPUS, DAY	Gwen and Jack stroll and talk	Jack, Gwen,	*EXTRAS*	
83		INT. UNIVERSITY CLASSROOM, DAY	Pregnant Gwen lectures students	Gwen	EXTRAS	
			2nd Meal: 2PM			
22		INT. UNIVERSITY CLASSROOM, DAY	Gwen finishes class, Jack visits as students leave	Gwen,Jack	EXTRAS	
3		INT. UNIVERSITY CLASSROOM, DAY	Jack practices lecture, Gwen walks in	Gwen, Jack		
			MOVE BACK TO LIGHTHOUSE RESORT FOR DINNER			

3rd Meal : 8PM

ADDITIONAL EQUIPMENT

PROPS/Pro Design

PROPS	dress classroom, murder pictures (power-point?), books, notepads

Wardrobe

Jack, Gwen

MAKE UP

Jack, Gwen

Special FX Make up

SPECIAL NOTES

HEAVY EXTRAS DAY, BE SURE TO HAVE RELEASE FORMS
CRAFTS SERVICES – ENOUGH FOR CREW AND EXTRAS
BREAKFAST, LUNCH AT LOCATION; DINNER AT RESORT

Producer:	Mamie Jean Calvert	Key PA	Tony Randolph
Exe Producer	Robert Calvert	PA	Rod Retamoza
Exe Producer	Jacqueline C. Reiland	PA	David Ferrero
Exe Producer	Witt Widmer	PA	Jeff Smith
Exe Producer	Judy Nessen	PA	Ryan Nelson
Exe Producer	Carolyn Munson		
Exe Producer	Jo Hoffmeier		
Assistant Producer	Linda Arslanian		
Co-Producer	Zach Thomson		
Co-Producer	Joel Fox		
Director	Louis Mandylor		
Director of Photography	Ted Caloroso		
Assistant Director	Serenity Pang-Bellman		
UPM	Charlene Agabao		
Script Supervisor	Judy Nessen		
Gaffer	Nghia Khuu		
1st Assistant Camera	Amy _______		
Best Boy	Samuel Kim		
Key Grip	Ryan Baustian		
Prouction Designer	Janene White		
Prop Master	John Ayers		
Wardrobe	Deborah		
Key make-up Artist	Barbara Mcgee		
SPFX make up Artist	JD Ayers		
Sound Mixer	Niko Zasimezuk		
Boom Operator	Jon Vennarucci		

Isleton Police Dept 100 2nd St, Isleton, CA (4.88 miles away) 916-777-7774	Isleton Fire Dept 201 2nd St, Isleton, CA (4.87 miles away) 916-777-7776	Antioch Convalescent Hospital 1210 A St, Antioch, CA (14.96 miles away) 925-757-8787

"In the Eyes of the Beholder"

PRODUCTION OFFICE:Cabin 1
ADDRESS:151 Brannan Island Rd
TELEPHONE NUMBER: (916) 370 5615

Director: *Louis Mandylor*
Producer: *Mamie Jean Colvert*
1st A.D.: *Serenity Pang-Bellman*

DAY 10 CALL SHEET

LOCATION: 151 Brannan Island Rd, Isleton, CA 95641-9767 PHONE: (916) 370-5615

Nov-25

CREW CALL ON LOCATION: 10AM **EST WRAP: 10PM**
Weather:

Sunrise: 6:42AM Sunset: 5PM

Sc No.	PG	Set	Synopsis	Character
42*		EXT. ARRIVING DOCK	Reverse POV Jack on boat, Gwen gets mad	Jack, Gwen
44		EXT. ARRIVING DOCK	Jack ties up boat	Jack
			COMPANY MOVE	
5		EXT. SALLY'S HOUSE	Gwen talks to Sally	Gwen, Sally
			COMPANY MOVE	
46		EXT. PHONE BOOTH, DAY	Gwen goes to phone booth to call Sam	Gwen
47*		EXT. PHONE BOOTH, DAY	Gwen talks to Sam on phone	Gwen
48*		EXT. PHONE BOOTH, DAY	Gwen calls Sam, sees Jack on speedboat	Gwen, Jack
50		EXT. PHONE BOOTH, DAY	Gwen finishes call, sees Mika chop fish	Gwen, Mika <-OMIT?
			2nd Meal: 3PM	
54		EXT. PHONE BOOTH, NIGHT	Gwen calls Sam, crying	Gwen
55		EXT. PHONE BOOTH, NIGHT	Gwen talks to Sam	Gwen

74a	EXT. PHONE BOOTH, NIGHT	Gwen sees phone line is cut, tries to wave to Dell and Earl; grabs knife	Gwen, Earl Dell	<-OMIT DELL AND EARL?
		COMPANY MOVE		
56	EXT. ARRIVING DOCK-YACHT	Kari goes overboard	Kari Stunt Double	

ADDITIONAL EQUIPMENT

PROPS/Pro Design

Production Design

Props knife, cut phone line, Kari's necklace, JD wig

Wardrobe

Jack, Gwen, Sally, Mika *Dell, Earl*

MAKE UP

Jack, Gwen, Sally, Mika *Dell, Earl*

Special FX Make up

JD WIG

LOCATION NOTES / PARKING

Parking is available in the resort.
QUIT PARKING ON LEVEE!!!!!!!!

SPECIAL NOTES

Divers, platform boat – JD NEEDS WIG, MUST SHAVE LEGS
DON'T FORGET SAM'S EYES

Producer: Mamie Jean Calvert		PA	Ron Bonomo
Exe Producer	Robert Calvert	PA	Rod Retamoza
Exe Producer	Jacqueline C. Reiland	PA	David Ferrero
Exe Producer	Witt Widmer	PA	Jeff Smith
Exe Producer	Judy Nessun	PA	
Exe Producer	Carolyn and Jo	PA	
Assistant Producer	Linda Arslanian		
Co-Producer	Joel Fox		
Director	Louis Mandylor		
Director of Photography	Ted Caloroso		
Assistant Director	Serenity Pang-Bellman		
UPM	Charlene Agabao		
Script Supervisor	Judy Nessun		
Gaffer	Nghia Khuu		
1st Assistant Camera	Amy Olk		
Best Boy	Samuel Kim		
Key Grip	Ryan Baustian		
Prouction Designer	Janene White		
Prop Master	John Ayers		
Wardrobe	Tamara		

Isleton Police Dept	Isleton Fire Dept	Antioch Convalescent Hospital
100 2nd St, Isleton, CA	201 2nd St, Isleton, CA	1210 A St, Antioch, CA
(4.88 miles away)	(4.87 miles away)	(14.96 miles away)
916-777-7774	916-777-7776	925-757-8787

IN THE EYES OF THE BEHOLDER- DAY 11 CALL SHEET

PRODUCTION OFFICE:Cabin 1
ADDRESS:151 Brannan Island Rd
TELEPHONE NUMBER: (916) 370 5615
DAY 11 CALL SHEET

Director: *Louis Mandylor*
Producer: *Mamie Jean Colvert*
1st A.D.: *Serenity Pang-Bellman*

LOCATION: 151 Brannan Island Rd, Isleton, CA 95641-9767 PHONE: (916) 370-5615

Nov-26

CREW CALL ON LOCATION: 10AM
Weather: 39F to 69F

EST WRAP: 10PM

Sunrise: 6:59AM Sunset: 4:48PM

Sc No.	PG	Set	Synopsis	Character	
23		EXT. ARRIVING DOCK	Jack and Gwen meet Bobby; Jack observes Gretchen, Bigler, Mamie, and extras	Jack, Gwen, Mamie, Bigler, Gretchen, Clarence	*EXTRAS*
24a		EXT. ARRIVING DOCK	Everyone arrives; Clarence greets them	Jack, Gwen, Gretchen, Bigler, Mamie, Clarence	*EXTRAS*
			COMPANY MOVE TO RESTAURANT		

2nd Meal: 4PM

27		INT. RESTAURANT	Jack and Gwen are waited on by Bobby	Jack, Gwen, Bobby	
29		INT. RESTAURANT	Jack knocks over a plate, everyone stares	Jack, Gwen, Mamie, Bigler, Gretchen	Kari, Donalds
53		INT. RESTAURANT	Jack drinks w/Kari and Donalds; Gretchen bartends	Jack, Gretchen	Kari, Donalds

PART 8

On The Set

AMERICAN
EAGLE

NO
SWIMMING
WADING
FROM DOCK
OR LAUNCH
RAMP

adidas

"IN THE EYES OF A KILLER"
ROLL
SCENE
TAKE
Director
LOUIS
IS IN A MOOD
Camera
MARK RUTLEDGE IS AWESOME
MOS DAY NITE
Date

04.20.55.26
A76
16
1
In the Eyes of the Beholder
L. Mandylor
12/02/07

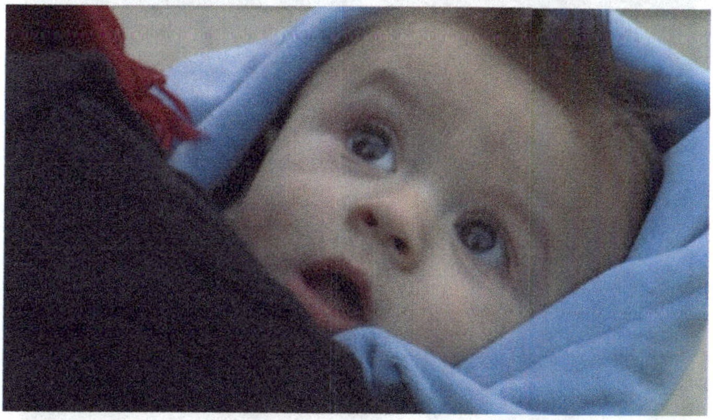

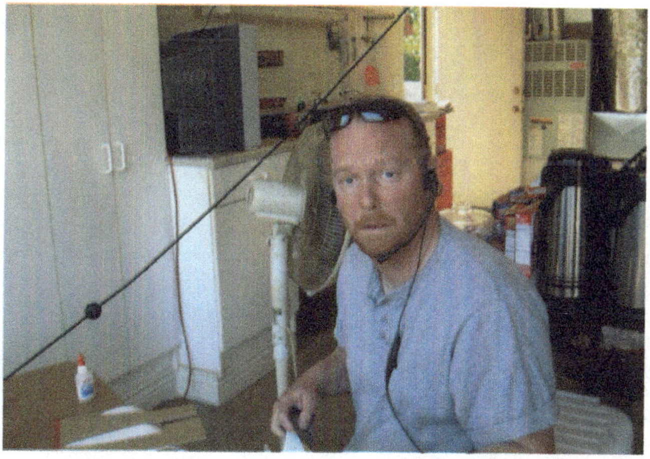

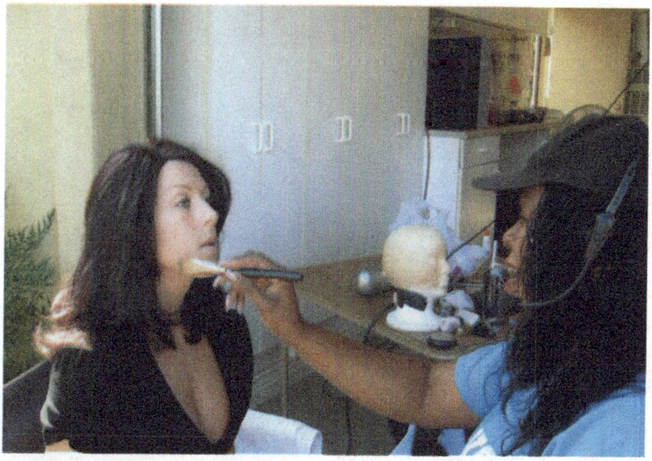

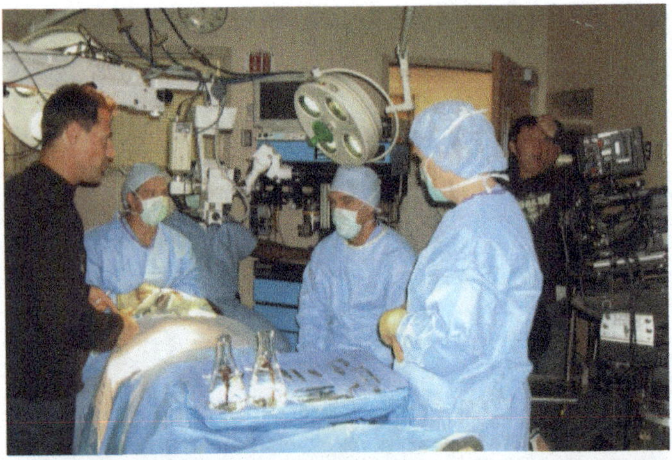

Home Cookin

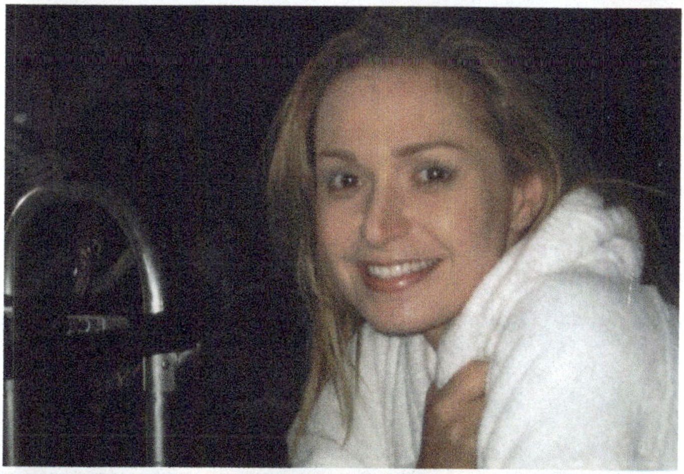

NCIS

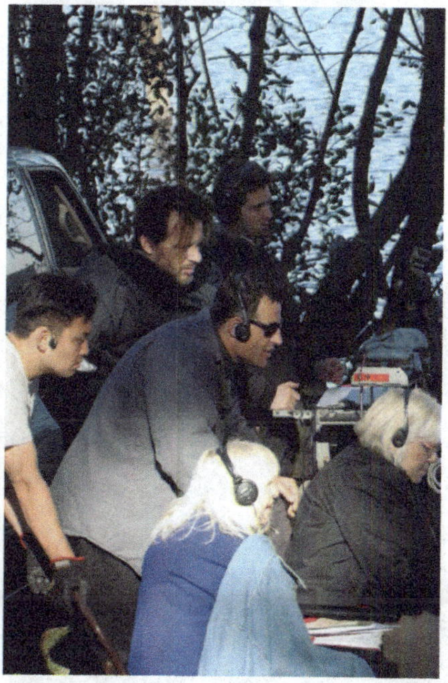

PART 9

Awards and Screenings

210
NORTH
Wrap Party
at
210 North Sierra Street
VIP pass - no cover
General pass - $10 cover

FACE

THANK YOU FOR COMING
AMBRA PRODUCTIONS
AND
KRAKATU FILMS

PART 10

Behind the Scenes: Elias Rieland's Story

Through his eight-year-old eyes, the ordinary became extraordinary, and a summer vacation became an unforgettable journey into the enchanting world of film production.

first

¶1 In my scrap book Once in a lifetime I would like to share with you my vacation, on a movie set. When I was on the movie set it was awsome. I met many new people, and saw some people that I already met. The coolest part was that I got to play a small roll in the movie

¶2 Now to get off my subject. I would like to tell you the plot of the movie. This movie is rated R so I would not suggest it to kids. Now the movie starts with a normal couple (But the husband is blind). As the couple are going through their relationship. The husband "Jack" decides to get an eye transplants to see again. So when Jack gets the transplant, he does not know the eyes were from a murderer. So as Jack and the wife "Gwen", go on the honey moon weird stuff starts to happen, like beating Gwen up and killing people. The confusing question is, will Jack ever be brought to justise, or will he be killed?!

boom Mead

Atti, Costa, and I

They shot some
of the movie where
my dad works. (Methodist hospital)

This was the yatch that they shot some of the movie at.

This was the Pool scene at my house. :)

This was at my House!
On the Set
This is the truck that carries everything!

Mamie, Barbra, and my mom.

Group shot

Actors

The actors were some of the most well rounded people you will ever meet. The first

PART 11

Blindsided

After *In the Eyes of a Killer* was out on the market, Monarch Pictures picked it up for pay-per-view, placement in video stores, etc. It was in 26,000 Walmart stores nationwide.

My mentor, Del Westen, after 10 years as owner of Action on Film (AOF), told me to pull the movie and rename it, put in some new footage, and add new music. This was to sell on the foreign market, and they wanted the poster to be orange. So *Blindsided* was born. It sold on many foreign markets and also sold under different titles.

An experimental transplant surgery has given Jack Newman the gift of sight. How he will use that gift will haunt you forever.
BLINDSIDED

Made in the USA
Monee, IL
16 May 2024

58535919R00213